We hope you enjoy this book.
Please return or renew it by the due date.
You can renew it at **www.norfolk.gov.uk/libraries**
app

Gay/t

RAT

PATRICE LAWRENCE

D0231550

OXFORD
UNIVERSITY PRESS

Barrington Stoke

Great Clarendon Street, Oxford, OX2 6DP, United Kingdom

Oxford University Press is a department of the University of Oxford.

It furthers the University's objective of excellence in research, scholarship, and education by publishing worldwide. Oxford is a registered trade mark of Oxford University Press in the UK and in certain other countries

© Patrice Lawrence 2021

Additional resources © Oxford University Press 2021

The moral rights of the author have been asserted

First published in 2021

All rights reserved. No part of this publication may be reproduced, stored in a retrieval system, or transmitted, in any form or by any means, without the prior permission in writing of Oxford University Press, or as expressly permitted by law, by licence or under terms agreed with the appropriate reprographics rights organization. Enquiries concerning reproduction outside the scope of the above should be sent to the Rights Department, Oxford University Press, at the address above.

You must not circulate this work in any other form and you must impose this same condition on any acquirer

British Library Cataloguing in Publication Data

Data available

ISBN 978-0-19-8494935

1 3 5 7 9 10 8 6 4 2

Paper used in the production of this book is a natural, recyclable product made from wood grown in sustainable forests.

The manufacturing process conforms to the environmental regulations of the country of origin.

Printed in China by Golden Cup

Acknowledgements

Cover: Oxford University Press / Shutterstock

The publisher would like to thank David Grant for writing the additional resources.

This book is dedicated to everyone who is doing their best in tough circumstances

Chapter 1

Al

I'm hungry. Really hungry. I want to fill the biggest bowl with cornflakes and then pile on sugar and milk and mix it all together. It doesn't have to be normal milk. Chocolate milk would be even better. I'd finish all the cornflakes and scrape the bowl until it squeaked. Then I'd munch down three slices of toast with peanut butter and chocolate spread, with a squished banana on top. After that, some crackers and cheese.

But all that food is in my head. I don't want to get off my bed and go into the kitchen because we haven't got no cornflakes, nor chocolate spread, nor cheese nor peanut butter. We've got milk, because Gran dropped it round. But I don't think we've got nothing I can pour milk over. We do have sugar, so maybe I can mix it into the milk and drink that instead.

There's another reason why I don't want to go into the kitchen. I'd have to pass Mum. She's on the sofa, in a mood. She's been trying not to have big moods since I started living with her again. We're supposed to be starting over. Mum's promised that she'll never go near the people that make her want to take drugs. She's promised that she'll never steal anything again. She's promised that it was the last time she'll go to prison. She's promised she'll make herself get better and strong. Mum didn't just promise me. She promised Gran and my social worker too. But I think she's finding it hard to keep her promises.

Her sad mood today is an extra big one. Mum didn't say nothing to me when I got home from school. She didn't even look at me when I made her a cup of tea. Her hand was all floppy over the arm of the sofa, so I put her mug on the table and pulled it towards her. I called her name – her real name, Ramona, not just Mum. She gave me a sort of smile and then went back to staring at the ceiling. I shouted her name, but Mum didn't say nothing more.

I started feeling cross, so I made myself do what Blessing, my social worker, says I should do when I want to kick off. *Breathe slowly, Al,* Blessing says, *and take yourself away from the thing that's making you upset.* So I came back into my bedroom and let out Venom and Vulture.

Venom and Vulture are my pet rats. They're not supposed to come out of their cage, because not everyone likes rats. But I do.

These are the reasons why people don't like rats:

1. They wee a lot.

2. They can get a bit smelly.

3. They carry diseases. (But these aren't any old rats. Venom and Vulture are posh rats from a pet shop. They got checked for fleas and plague.)

4. They eat anything.

Mum says I'm not supposed to have my rats here at all, but as long as I behave myself, she'll let me keep them. I got Venom and Vulture from Maya, who was staying in the same foster home as me.

There have been lots of times when Mum hasn't been able to look after me. When I was small, I'd move in with my dad or my gran. But last time Gran told the social workers she couldn't have me because she'd be in New Zealand visiting her sister, and my dad wouldn't take me in neither.

I haven't been to my dad's for three years now. He moved out of London with his third family. (I'm from his second family.) Dad's new girlfriend is called Lara and they have twins called Bianca and Marsha. Dad says that Lara's hands are too full with the twins for me to stay there now.

So I ended up with Macey and Lee, foster parents who look after teenagers in an emergency. That means kids like me and Maya who haven't got nowhere else to go. Macey didn't mind rats, but Lee hated them. Once, Venom stuck her claw out from her cage and hooked the scarf Macey had been knitting for Lee's mother. Venom pulled the scarf into her cage and we only noticed when half the scarf had been unravelled and turned back into wool.

Lee told the social workers that the rats had to go. I was moving back with Mum by then and I promised I'd care for them.

I let Venom climb up my leg. She used to hang from my sleeve with her teeth. She's getting fat and heavy now, so I won't let her do it so much in case she falls and hurts herself. Vulture is sniffing around my room like she thinks there's food hidden behind the walls. Watching her just makes me feel more hungry, so I put them both back in their cage.

I slump back onto my bed and open up the Argos catalogue Gran left here. I find the pages with all the games consoles. Dad says he's gonna buy me one for my birthday, but he said the same thing last Christmas. Mum says I'm gonna be an old man before I get that gift.

I rip the pages out. Then I tear them into tiny pieces. I feel better for a few minutes and then my stomach groans so loud it almost makes the catalogue shake.

I need food!

I need food right now.

I'm gonna do it. I'm gonna get the milk.

I open my bedroom door slowly, go out into the hall and look into the sitting room. Mum isn't in there no more. I hear the fridge open in the kitchen. Good. I want her to know we haven't got no food, because she's promised the social workers that she'll make sure I'm all right. I know she doesn't want to break her promises.

These are the promises Mum made when social services said we were allowed to live together again:

1. Mum would give up her bad friends.

2. She would make sure we always had food and it was going to be healthy.

3. She would stop smoking. She doesn't smoke inside, but it's bad for her and expensive.

4. She would use the money she saves from not smoking to buy fruit and vegetables.

I know Mum's trying to keep the promises, even if she hasn't given up smoking. And she hasn't bought masses of vegetables, but I don't mind that.

"Mum!" I shout.

She comes out of the kitchen and she's wearing her big coat. I look out of the window. It wasn't raining when I came back from school. I'd been too hot and took off my blazer on the bus. I almost left it there because I hate wearing a blazer, but Gran bought it and she'd go mad if I lost it. There's only so much mad that I want to make Gran.

Mum doesn't need an enormous coat like that in this weather. So why's she wearing it? I think about the coat's deep pockets. There's even a pocket hidden inside the lining. Pockets where you can hide things.

Mum says, "I'm going out, Al. You need to stay here."

"Where are you going?" I ask.

"I'm just going to ... going to see a friend."

Mum hasn't got no friends who live nearby. That's why we moved all the way over here. The social worker says it makes Mum's life easier to be far away from all the bad friends that made her go to prison.

Mum goes over to the shoe rack and slips on her trainers. I run over and put mine on too.

"Who are you going to see?" I ask.

Mum won't meet my eyes.

Please don't break your promises, Mum, I think. I don't know what's worse. Mum really going to see the friends she's not supposed to see or Mum not going to see friends at all in her coat with the secret pocket.

"Mum!" I shout. "Tell me!"

She looks me in the eye and says, "OK, Al. I'm not going to see my friends. I'm going to get us some food."

Just the word "food" makes my hunger go twisty again.

"Then I can come with you," I say.

"No, Al. Stay here."

"I can help you carry—"

"I'm not getting that much," Mum tells me. "I don't need help."

Her eyes have dropped away from mine again.

"You're not really going shopping, are you?" I say. "That's why you don't want me to come with you. You promised you wouldn't do rubbish stuff no more! You're not allowed to keep letting me down!"

Mum's eyes snap back up to me. "You're hungry, Al," she says. "The fridge is empty. I'm going to get some food, right?"

I thought she was gonna shout. But her words are all flat like they've been stomped on.

Mum opens the front door and slams it shut behind her.

Chapter 2

Mum

I count to sixty in my head, then I open the door and check outside. I can't see Mum. I go back inside, put on my trainers and make sure I have my door key in my pocket. Then I leave, closing the front door behind me gently.

This is the third place me and Mum have lived since she came out of prison. She says, "Third time lucky." We got chucked out of the first place because the landlord wanted his rent and Mum didn't have her benefits yet to pay it. After that, the council put us in one of those places that no one else wants. The flat next door had been burned out, and one weekend people broke in and had a party. There was loud music and glass smashing and people running up and down the balcony shouting. Sometimes they banged on our window and door.

Mum put on some music to drown out the noise, but she wouldn't turn it down again after the party had finished. She played her music all Monday and all Tuesday until the neighbours in the flat above us called the police. They told Mum to turn it down and she did. But not long after, she turned it up again.

I called Blessing, my social worker, who came round and calmed Mum down. She told Mum that no child should live in a place like that and helped Mum apply for the flat we live in now.

This flat doesn't look special, but it is. The council cleaned it before we came in, so we didn't have to deal with the rubbish from the last people. In the place the landlord chucked us out from, I opened a cupboard and a load of plastic bags full of empty cans fell onto my head. There was a cooker, but Mum wouldn't use the oven because she said it smelled like a fish had died in there.

This place is bigger too. Mum even has her own bedroom, so she doesn't have to sleep on the sofa. Blessing made sure we've got a proper cooker and a fridge, and Gran gave us her old microwave. We use that more than the cooker. The bathroom isn't mouldy – well, not much. The housing officer told us that the old woman in the flat above left her bath running and it came down through our ceiling. That happened before we lived here, but there's a stain above the window that looks like a vulture with one of its wings spread out.

I don't know if the old woman still lives above us. We don't hear nothing from up there. It's the idiot in the flat below that I hate. Blessing says that "hate" is a bad word. She wasn't happy with me saying "idiot" neither. But that's what Mr Brayker is. An idiot. And I hate him.

The first week we were here, Mr Brayker called the council every day saying that Mum's music was too loud. I know it was him, because he came up and knocked on our door first. He said that if Mum didn't turn the racket down, he'd make sure there was trouble.

I tried to tell Mum that she didn't need to blast her music so loud, because there weren't any parties next door. But Mum said music makes her feel happy. After me, music is what she missed most in prison.

A woman from the council told Mum that she was being anti-social and she would have to move out if she didn't turn the music down. After the woman left, Mum turned the volume up even higher, just for a few seconds. I was standing by the window and touched the glass. It was shaking.

*

Everything is quiet on our block today. I run down the stairs from the flat and out onto the street. I can't see Mum.

There are two supermarkets near us. The closest one is pretty small and a man stays outside, watching me whenever I go in. There's another man inside who stays by the freezers, looking at me when I'm walking around.

The other shop is by the main road. It's much bigger. Mum says it isn't any cheaper, but no one stares at us in there. If she really is going shopping, that's where she'll be.

I weave around all the kids trying to get into the newsagent under our flats. I'm so hungry, I want to run into the shop, sweep up an armful of sweets and shove them all into my mouth. But instead I cross the road and cut across the grassy patch between two tall tower blocks. I come out into a car park. I step over the chain fence and I can see the big supermarket opposite. And there's Mum, just going inside.

Right. So Mum's telling the truth about going out for food. I can just go home and wait for her to bring back a big bag full of goodies. Cornflakes and beef burgers and cheese and jam. Chocolate milk and orange juice, but not the stuff with "juicy bits" in it. They're not juicy. They taste like jumper fluff.

I should just go home. Mum hates people checking up on her all the time. But my feet are making me cross the road and follow Mum into the shop.

Mum's not by the fruit and vegetables. She isn't near the fresh pizzas, nor the baskets of muffins and bread rolls. And I don't see her near the ham and cheese. There are some fridges at the back. Maybe she's getting some of them special chocolate puddings. Gran bought some for us the day Mum came out of prison. I took a really long time eating mine because I didn't want the taste to go away.

I pass the fridges with the meat. Most of the meat has got yellow alarm stickers on it. The first time I came in here, I saw a girl pick up some burgers and run out. No one chased her, even when the alarm bleeped. But I don't need to even think about doing that. I can just ask Mum to buy the burgers for us.

I run my fingers across all the different burgers and choose a pack where the burgers are so thick they're almost bursting out of the plastic. I rub my belly. *Wait*, I say to it. *You're gonna be filled up soon.*

I walk to the end of the shelves, then go back and check where I've just been. There's Mum! She's looking at cheese and there's a basket by her feet. I strain to see what's in it. There are two tins of tomatoes. I don't know why we need those. I hate them. A big box of Weetabix and some eggs. She's got washing powder too, even though Gran gave us some.

Mum picks up some cheese and then ... I don't see her put it down again. She doesn't put it in the basket. I look at her hand and the basket again. Did she put it back? *Please, please, Mum!* I think. *You've just put it back, right?*

"Mum?" The last word must have come out of my mouth because she looks around.

"Al!" Mum says, turning to face me. "Go home!"

Her coat is unbuttoned in the middle, just enough for her to reach her secret pocket.

"I've ... I've come to help you!" I say.

"I don't need help."

Mum buttons up her coat. Her face is shiny, like she's been sweating. She doesn't need that coat! It's not cold. I think about the secret pocket and the cheese that disappeared. My heart hurts.

I move closer to Mum and keep my voice low. "Please come home with me," I say.

She glances at me, then around the shop. "Go home, Al!" Mum tells me. "I won't be long."

I touch her arm. "I know what you're doing. You don't need to. We'll be OK."

Mum shakes her head. "We won't," she says. "It's the only way. I can't ask your gran again and ... They say our money's gonna be here soon. This will be the only time. I promise." Mum sees the burgers I'm holding. "Go and put them back, Al. We don't need them."

I look down at her basket. "Is this for us too? I hate tinned tomatoes."

She hands me the basket and says, "You put all this back and I'll wait outside for you."

I open my mouth to reply, but Mum starts walking away from me towards the exit. And then, for the first time ever, I see there's a security guard. He's got one of them faces that looks like someone bigger has just had a go at him and now he's ready to bully someone small. There was a kid like that in my last school. He was called Federer. He was always ready and waiting for the best time to jump on me. And, man, this guard looks like he's ready to jump.

I swallow hard. I want to call Mum's name and stop her walking out, but then the security guard would know there's something wrong. I pass the meat fridge again. The bright yellow alarm stickers seem to blink at me. Alarm. ALARM! When Mum walks out of that door, there's going to be a siren sound and that security guard will grab Mum and ...

It's too late. She's walking past the guard. One step. Another step. Outside, the traffic lights have made the cars wait. Everything is quiet. Even my hunger doesn't feel so sharp now. Mum takes another step and the door swishes open.

The alarm! *The alarm, Mum!*

She's going out of the door. The security guard's stepping towards her and ... he's just waving to a woman in one of the cars. The traffic lights turn green and the cars zoom past again. The alarm didn't go off.

I breathe out even though I didn't know I was holding my breath. I dump the basket on the floor and race after Mum.

Just as I reach the door, a voice shouts, "You haven't paid for that!"

What?

"See!" the voice says. "That boy's going to steal from you!"

I turn round and see a man standing by the meat fridge. He's pointing at me but looking at the security guard. I know that man. I've seen him when he's knocked on our door and told Mum to turn down her music. It's Brayker, from the flat below.

Mum's outside, but she's turned around. She's staring at me through the glass. I want to shake my head and tell her to carry on walking. I'll be all right. I haven't stolen anything. Everyone can see that.

The security guard starts walking towards me. His boots clump down hard. Yeah, he would have been the kid who stood on your hand when you were getting up after school assembly. The guard is smiling like he can hear the sound of crunching fingers in his head already.

"I haven't done nothing!" I shout.

The guard's still smiling and his hand shoots out like he's going to grab me.

"Don't you dare!" The doors swish open and Mum steams back into the shop. "Take your hands off my boy!" she says.

I try to say, "It's OK, Mum," but my words are slower than her. She's rushing towards us and ... and she doesn't stop.

Mum's arms are out like she's coming to hug me, but the guard steps in front of her. I think she means to push him away. But she pushes him too hard. I hear a thump like the sound when I punch the pillow with anger. I want to squeeze my eyes shut, but I also want to see at the same time. The guard's on the floor and he's rubbing the back of his head. He must have hit it on the fridge.

The guard shouts. No. It's a different guard. Where did he come from? It's like he's jumped out of one of the freezers just to grab Mum's arm.

"I know my rights," Mum yells. "You can't touch me. I haven't done anything!"

"I saw everything!" That's Brayker. He's holding on to the fridge like he's so happy, he can't stand up.

A swear word falls out of my mouth, one that Blessing said I should never say. But I don't believe in "never". Not when a big guard has grabbed my mum's arm. I dive forward, but someone grabs me. I try to wriggle, but they're not letting go. I start shouting, but then I stop.

Mum's sort of hanging from the guards. She looks like all her bones have slid out of her. Her mouth is open and she's shaking her head really slowly. She's not looking at me. She's looking past me at the police car that's just parked up outside. It must have been on its way back to the police station on the other side of the park. I wish Mum had never said her promises out loud, because it's like the world's decided that she's not allowed to keep them. How else did the police get here so fast?

The police officers get out of the car – a woman and a man. Then I realise that I'm sinking, just like Mum. The man who's holding me lets go and steps away from me. I fall onto the floor. Mum comes alive again. She pulls herself free from the guards and crouches down beside me and looks into my eyes.

"Al?" Mum says.

"I'm OK, Mum. My legs went wobbly."

As Mum helps me up, I can see bulges under her coat. They're going to find her secret pocket.

But maybe that doesn't even matter now, not after she pushed the guard. He's still on the floor and the policeman is crouched next to him. The guard's rubbing his head and pointing at Mum.

The policewoman says, "Is that your mum?"

I realise she's talking to me and I nod.

She asks me my name and I tell her.

"We're all going up to the manager's office, Al," the policewoman says.

She's waiting and I realise "we" means me too.

The policeman takes Mum's arm and they start walking towards the back of the shop. Mum's moving like one of them toys that are running out of battery.

I don't understand! They shouldn't be taking us anywhere! Mum was already outside. I'd put the basket down. I wasn't stealing anything.

"Shall I take these, Al?" the policewoman says.

I look down at my hands. They're still holding the burgers. I look back up and see Brayker. He's still standing by the fridges, watching. I want to throw the burgers at him as hard as I can. I want to be like Thor with his hammer and send Brayker out through the wall and into the park. But my hands just flop and the burgers fall onto the floor. The policewoman sighs and picks them up.

Chapter 3

Gran

Gran picks me up from the police station. She couldn't get to the shop earlier when the police called, so I had to come here with Mum.

A policewoman tries to talk to me, but all I want is Mum. I'm not allowed to see her yet. I have to breathe in and out loads of times. I breathe so hard that my whole head fills with air. I'm supposed to imagine the breath pushing out all my anger. It works a bit, because I don't swear or kick anything, but I still feel mad about everything. It's like hot bubbles behind my eyes.

Gran isn't happy, neither. I'm not sure if it's with me or Mum. Gran says I'm to come with her. I don't want to leave Mum at the police station, but I can tell by Gran's voice that I better not argue.

Gran stops off at the drive-thru MacDonald's as she says she doesn't have any food in her house that I'll like. I'm not allowed to eat it yet as it will make Gran's car smell. Instead, I have to listen to her saying bad things about Mum.

These are some of the things Gran says:

1. I'm disappointed.

2. I don't want to give up on my only daughter, but enough is enough.

3. I won't always be around to pick up the pieces.

4. Ramona should think about her son before getting back into her old ways.

When we get back to Gran's house, I sit in the kitchen eating my burger and listen to Gran call up my aunties and say the same things over and over again. I've got to eat the burger off a plate because Gran says it's bad manners to eat out of boxes.

I don't want to be mean about Gran. I know kids who haven't got no one in their family who wants to help out. And some kids don't know if they've got any family at all. But I don't want to take nothing from Gran, because it's gonna come with a lecture. I shouldn't have let her buy this burger, but I've got to eat.

Each bite makes me feel guilty. I didn't check Venom and Vulture's water earlier. I think there was some left in their bottle, but Venom gets really thirsty. As I'm washing up the plate, I wonder if I can sneak out. I can't tell Gran I've got a thirsty rat to look after. If she knew that Mum let me keep rats in my bedroom, she'd send me away to be adopted.

I'm trying to figure out what to do just as Gran comes into the kitchen. She's holding up her phone like she thinks I can see the other person she's talking to, but she isn't on a video call.

"You'll be going home tonight, Al," Gran says.

Good. I try to keep my mouth from smiling. I don't want Gran's "*Al, you should be grateful I'm here to pick up the pieces again*" lecture. But then my smile breaks out anyway.

"So Mum's coming home!" I say.

Gran crouches down in front of me. She's not an old-looking grandma. She had my mum when she was a teenager, then she worked really hard to get a good job. I know that because Gran's told me. A lot of times.

Gran's got long black hair with a white curl just above her ear. Her eyebrows are thin and I can't help looking at the tiny holes around them where she pulled out the hair. Her skin's light brown. Mine isn't brown at all. I look white, like my dad. Gran once showed me an old picture of us in the park when I was about three. She said that people used to think Gran was my childminder.

"Sorry, Al," Gran says. "Your mum's not coming home tonight."

I look at Gran. Her face is tight and serious. She brushes her white curl away and it pings back. Her head moves forward like she wants to kiss my forehead, then she pulls back and laughs.

"Sometimes I forget that you're not a baby any more," Gran says. "I can't just plant a smacker on your face and pretend it's ..."

She doesn't finish. I know what she's gonna say. *And pretend it's all OK.* It was easy to pretend when I was younger, before I knew what a broken promise was.

Gran stands up. "Plum's agreed to stay over with you tonight and then—"

"Plum?" I say.

"Your sister."

"I know who she is."

Gran shoots me her "*don't-give-me-attitude*" look.

My social workers describe Plum as my *half* sister. She's from Dad's first family with his first wife, Shauna. Dad used to bring Plum round sometimes when I stayed with him, and she'd boss me around loads.

"Why's Plum coming?" I ask. "I haven't seen her in ages."

"Because I asked your father if you could go to him," Gran says. "But he said ..." Gran flicks her curl again. "He said he can't come and get you right now. I was happy to take you to him, but he called Plum instead. Your dad said ..." Gran makes a face. "Plum's got a new job and it's easier for her to get there from your flat. Is that OK with you, Al?"

No! It's not OK. It should be Mum with me, not Plum. But what's the point telling Gran? It's already decided.

"Your life's been turned upside down so many times," Gran says. "If Plum comes, it means you won't miss school if ... if everything isn't sorted out with your mum quickly. I'll make sure you're OK for food. That way you'll stay close to your friends, too."

I almost smile. Gran doesn't know that my only friends are called Venom and Vulture and live in my bedroom.

"Will Mum be back tomorrow?" I ask.

Gran squeezes her lips together, then she says, "We have to be prepared in case she's away for longer. That security guard ... He says your mum hit him. It's not good."

"She didn't! It was an accident!" I say.

"I know you're upset, Al," Gran says. "But please don't shout."

It feels like the bubbles of anger are trying to push themselves out of my head into my skin. I breathe and breathe and breathe. But it doesn't help. My face is hot and my feet are twitching like they want to kick out. So I try to imagine something else. Venom and Vulture. They're at home and they need me.

"I've called a lawyer," Gran says. "One who knows your mum. Maybe she can convince the police to release your mum while they decide if they're going to press charges. But ..." Gran sighs. "Your mum's out of prison on licence. That means that she can go straight back in if she does anything wrong. I think ... I think pushing a security guard and being caught shoplifting is definitely doing something wrong."

I think of the security guard rubbing his head and pointing at Mum. Yeah, he's gonna make sure Mum has the hardest time. Then I think of Brayker standing by the fridge watching us like we were his favourite film. My bubbles of anger are pushing harder to get out.

Mum and I were all right until Brayker stuck his ugly nose in. He's probably got a massive fridge full of food. He doesn't care that we haven't. He just wants us to go away. Maybe he even followed us to the shop so he could get us in trouble.

Well, Brayker is going to find something out. You don't mess with Al and his mum.

*

Plum can't come to the flat straight away, so I have to wait for her at Gran's. I'm starting to be what Gran calls "antsy". And, yeah, that is the right word for how I feel.

When I was six, I tried to do a sliding tackle against this older kid who kept fouling me. But I slid into an ants' nest. Man, those ants weren't happy. They bit me all over. The football coach said that the poor ants were only protecting their eggs. That didn't help me, and I told him so with all the swear words I knew. It wasn't the coach whose T-shirt was full of crawling and biting bugs. They were even running through my hair. I had to take off nearly all my clothes in the park.

The coach told Gran I wasn't allowed to come back to the football club because I'd sworn at him. I hadn't meant to. The bites hurt and the words just came out.

Now I'm feeling a kind of tickly, crawly feeling going up and down my arms and legs. I can't sit still, so I walk round Gran's sitting room, picking up all the photos and looking at them. Gran's watching me, but she doesn't say nothing.

There's a photo of me in my buggy with Gran and her boyfriend, Ethan. And there's Mum in her Year 6 class photo. Mum's standing right behind the teacher and grinning. If you look really carefully, you can just see the tips of Mum's fingers doing a peace sign over the teacher's head.

There are pictures of Gran's other children too. They're both at university and don't really have much to do with Mum, so I ignore these photos. I pick up a little china hedgehog. It's painted to look all spiky, but when I hold it to my cheek it feels smooth and cold.

Finally, the doorbell goes. I place the hedgehog carefully back on the shelf and I hear Gran breathe out.

"That must be Plum," Gran says.

Plum's nineteen. It's weird because even though she's older than me, we still look alike. Mum says Dad must have super-power genes, because all his children have got his long nose and small chin. I don't think my chin's grown since I was two.

Plum has darker skin, like her mum, and she's twisted her hair into bunches. Both her ears are so full of earrings I can't see much skin. There's a ring through the middle of Plum's nose. Gran keeps frowning at it like she thinks the ring's gonna notice and drop out by itself.

Plum gives me a little nod and says, "Sorry about your mum, Al."

"Yeah," I reply.

Gran goes into the kitchen to make some tea. We follow her in.

"I've made up a box of food," Gran says. "If ... if it turns out the police are going to keep Ramona for longer, I'll book in a grocery delivery." Gran's talking to Plum like this stuff isn't important to me too.

Then Gran does turn to me. "Plum's studying hard for her exams as well as working. Please don't give her stress." Her white curl pings again. "I really don't want social services involved. They're too busy already."

"Al's all right," Plum says to me. "Aren't you?"

I'm not. But if I get to stay with Venom and Vulture, I'll try to be all right for Plum.

*

Gran drops us home with the box of food. If she'd given it to us earlier, Mum wouldn't be at the police station. As we're getting out of the car, I look up. Our window is dark and empty, but Brayker's light is on. He hasn't drawn his curtains and he's at the window, looking down on us. I can't see his smile, but I know it's there.

Plum and Gran go into the sitting room and whisper about keys and homework and how to use the washing machine. I know all that stuff, but nobody asks me. It's like they still want me to think that Mum might be home tomorrow.

I go into my bedroom and finally check on Venom and Vulture. They're in a corner of the cage huddled together like they're telling each other secrets. I want to take them out, but I better wait for Gran to leave first. When I go back to the sitting room, Gran gives me a lecture about how I have to behave. Plum doesn't say nothing, but she looks at me like she's on my side.

"I know I'm going on about this," Gran says. "But your mum told me in the police station that it's the man in the flat underneath you that called the security guard in the shop. He's the one your mum upset when she was playing her music too loud. I do not want you to be at war with your neighbours, Al. If you do anything the council think is wrong, they will come down hard. And you and your mum will end up worse off. Do you understand?"

"Brayker started it," I say.

"No, Al," Gran replies. "It hurts me to say this, but your mum started it by blasting the poor man out of his flat with her music. You have to be considerate. You have no idea what's going on in other people's lives."

I don't say nothing.

"Do you understand me, Al?" Gran asks.

I nod, because I understand. But it doesn't mean my mind's changed. I'm still gonna make Brayker sorry.

Gran leaves at last and Plum goes into Mum's room. There's not much in it – just a bed and the rail for her clothes. Plus a stool we found by the bin chutes that Mum uses as a table. Plum looks at the bed and the heap of pillows and duvet. The duvet hasn't got no cover on it because Mum sometimes forgets to put one on when she's in a mood.

"Do you know where the clean bed stuff is?" Plum asks.

"Yeah," I say. "It's in the drawers in my room." I go back, pull out a bright red cover and take it in to Plum.

"Fiery," she laughs. "Can you give us a hand?"

I help Plum spread the cover out on the floor, then we feed the duvet in. I wriggle inside the cover and make sure the corners of the duvet match up.

"We need a sheet too," Plum says. "To go on top of the mattress."

There's one on the bed already, but I suppose Plum wants a different one. I head back to my bedroom, but Plum overtakes me. My mouth opens.

I want to shout at her to stop. No one but Mum's allowed to go in there. Mum promised me. It's my room, just mine.

But it's not just mine. It's Venom and Vulture's room too.

I rush in after Plum. She hasn't screamed yet, but sometimes you can be too scared to scream. It's like your body's been dropped in freezing chemicals. Your mouth opens, but all your sounds are frozen too.

Maybe Plum hasn't seen the cage. It's nearly as tall as me, but Mum says sometimes people only see what they want to see.

But no, Plum's standing right in front of the cage. She's seen it. She's not moving. She's frozen.

She turns round to look at me.

"Cute," Plum says. "But the council are going to kick you out if they find out. You know that?"

"Y ... yeah."

"Don't worry, I'm not going to tell them," Plum says. "But that's why you have to behave yourself, Al. I know you're mad at Mr Brayker, but there's loads of people who need flats like this. Your mum's already been told to turn her music down. The council are going to think you're troublemakers and if you're not careful, you'll get yourselves chucked out."

I wonder what will happen if Mum stays in prison. If she's not here, will the council decide we don't need the flat no more? I think about Brayker in the supermarket and just now, watching us come in. I'm getting angrier. I should hold it back, but it's hard. It's not the hot-bubble angry but the creeping angry. It's like when my trainers get leaky and my socks are stuck to my toes and the rain's crawling up and up. Brayker's the troublemaker. He's the one who's trying to get us chucked out. There's no way I'm gonna let him get away with it.

"In here?" Plum asks.

"What?" I say.

She's standing by the drawers. All the sheets and stuff are coming out from when I was looking for the duvet cover. I nod and Plum pulls out a corner of something. A big lump of clothes lands on the floor. I hold it while Plum untangles a sheet. She takes it into Mum's bedroom and I close my door after her.

I push my nose against Venom and Vulture's cage. Mum won't get that near to them. She says they're too stinky and she needs a nose clip, but I know humans who smell worse.

"Plum seems all right," I say to them. "She wasn't even scared of you. But ... she needs to understand. I have to do this for Mum's sake."

I drop my blanket over their cage. I don't think rats are scared by loud noises. If they are, I don't think my blanket will help that much, but still.

I find the playlist Mum downloaded for me on my computer. I've got her speakers. She asked me to look after them to stop her being tempted to use them.

That doesn't matter now.

I plug the speakers in to the computer, then I tip them both over so they're facing the floor. Mum likes these speakers because the bass has power. She says it's like a giant's footsteps.

I scroll down the songs in my phone and find "Another One Bites The Dust" by Queen. The boom, boom, boom bit at the beginning is the best. Mum says that when I was a baby, she used to give me a wooden spoon so I could bash a saucepan along with it. I don't need a saucepan now. I can jump, high in the air, and slam my feet down hard.

I make sure the speakers and my computer are turned up to the highest volume. Then I press "play".

Boom! Boom! Boom! go Queen.

Bang! Bang! Bang! go my feet on the floor.

I wish I could jump even harder. I wish I could roll away the carpet so there's nothing hiding the sound. I hope it's right over Brayker's head and his ears hurt and his head wants to explode.

My door slams open and Plum rushes in.

"What the hell are you doing?" Plum asks.

Then suddenly there's nothing. No sound. No light. Just me and Plum standing there in the silence and dark.

Chapter 4

Venom and Vulture

"Your power's on a key, right?" Plum asks. "It's pay as you go?"

"Yes," I say.

"Do you know when your mum last topped it up?"

"No."

Plum sighs. My eyes have adjusted to the dark and I can see her now. She looks pretty cross. "We'd better go and top it up, then."

She makes me unplug my computer and take the speakers back into Mum's room. I have to go out with her too. Plum says she can't trust me by myself. She tops up the electric key at the Al-Nisa shop across the road and gives it to me to bring home while Plum goes to apologise to Brayker. She's going to try to persuade him not to report me to the council and she really doesn't want me there with her.

I stomp up the stairs and go into the dark flat. I slot the key back into the meter and the fridge starts humming and the light comes on.

I shut my bedroom door and let Venom and Vulture out of their cage. They chase each other round my room, then go and hide under my bed. Mum says I have to be careful that they don't try to eat the mattress. I've checked and there's a few nibble marks but nothing too bad. Mum's never going to see those.

There's a knock on my door. I open it to Plum, step out and close it behind me. Plum moves towards me.

"I think we need to understand each other," she says.

I lean back on the door and stare at my feet. I don't have to listen to her. She isn't my mum.

"Al?" Plum says.

I don't answer.

"Look at me!" she shouts.

I make my head lift up but keep my eyes down.

Plum sighs. "I'm not your mum. I get it. And I'm not your teacher. But I'm doing you a big favour. If I'm not here, they're going to send you to foster care. Do you understand?"

Of course I do, but I shrug.

"And you think you can take your pets with you?" Plum asks.

This time I stare at her.

"I don't make the rules, Al," she says. "But if you want to stay here with your rats, you're going to have to stop acting like an idiot. When your mum's back, you can do what you want."

I say, "When is Mum coming back?"

Plum makes a face. I don't think she knows she's doing it. I think she's trying to work out what to say to me.

"I don't know," Plum says. "Your gran's going down the police station tomorrow and she's going to let us know when there's any news."

I shrug again. I do that when I don't know what to do with my body.

Plum makes another face. "I'm on your side, you know. It's really crap, what's happened to your mum, but it's just as crap if you give me grief about it. And it's going to be even more crap if you get yourself chucked out of the flat."

I go back into my room. For Plum's sake, I don't bang the door.

Plum knocks and opens the door a crack. "And I bought some chips," she says. "If you want them, they're in the kitchen."

She closes my door again. I do want chips. But not now. I lie down on my bed. I want to think of good things, but my head is full of Mum and the way she went all floppy when the police car came. I don't even know if she's still in the police station. What if they've already taken her straight back to prison?

I try to imagine what Mum's thinking. I hope she's not angry with me because I didn't stay at home like she'd asked. I wish she'd just told me that she didn't have any money. But I have to remember that it's not Mum's fault. It's Brayker's.

I close my eyes and think a "goodnight" as hard as I can. Maybe, wherever Mum is, she'll feel it.

*

I wake up because something's eating my ear. It hurts and I yell.

"Al?" Plum flings the door open. "Are you OK?"

Plum turns on the light. Something runs across my pillow, flips off my bed and darts past Plum into the sitting room. Of course! Venom was having a midnight ear snack. I'd forgotten to put my rats back in their cage. Vulture chases after her. Plum swears.

"Catch them, Al! In case they get out of the flat!"

I push myself off the bed. Plum has already closed the door to Mum's bedroom and the bathroom. I race over and close the kitchen door. They could get under the cooker or behind the fridge or into a cupboard. My rats might find a pipe to escape through.

But they're on the sofa. Venom's crouched on a cushion looking like Spiderman when he's just landed. Vulture is lying across the back of the sofa like she's too tired to move. I really do need to put her on a diet.

Plum watches me as I pick them up and stuff them both down the front of my jumper. I can feel them twitching against my T shirt and it makes me feel calm. I take them into my room and let them plop back into their cage. Plum's behind me, watching me, so I make sure I close the cage's hatch and test it afterwards to show it's locked.

"Right," Plum says. "That's another reason why you're lucky it's me here. Everybody else I know would be so damn freaked out by that. I have to finish an essay for college now. I really can't be disturbed."

Plum bangs out of my room and into Mum's. I close my door, but I don't turn off the light. My brain's bubbling like my stomach does when I'm hungry. I know I'm never going back to sleep again. I jam in my earbuds and listen to Mum's playlist. It makes my brain move round even faster. I turn the music off and lie there. Brayker's bedroom might be right below mine. He's probably lying in his bed snoring, without a care at all.

I lie there and think. And think. And think. Every thought has Brayker in it.

I check the time on my phone. It's nearly half past one in the morning. I'm never gonna sleep with Brayker stuck in my head. I have to do something.

I creep out of bed, open my bedroom door and wait. Venom scratches on the cage. I hold my finger to my mouth, but I don't dare go "shhh" in case Plum hears. Venom must understand, because she stops scratching. I go back and drop the blanket over the cage just in case.

The sitting room is dark and I can't see any light beneath Mum's door. Plum must be asleep. Good.

I edge over to the kitchen and open the fridge. The light in there doesn't work, so I don't have to worry. I open the box of eggs that Gran gave us and take one out. Yeah, it would be good to have it for breakfast, but what I need it for now is better.

I hold the egg carefully in the palm of my hand and go into the hall. I have to be quick, so I don't put on shoes. I take my keys off the hook and leave the flat.

It's bright outside. There's a row of streetlights down by the car park and all the lights along the balcony are on too. Our block's an L-shape, so I can see some of the flats below.

A front door opens on the first floor. I stand still and squint my eyes, but I can't see who's come out. Maybe they're going to do something bad too. They rush along the balcony to the stairs at the end of the block. They haven't seen me. I have to be quick in case they come back again or someone else turns up.

I run down the stairs to the next floor. The cold concrete makes my toes curl. I turn the corner of the block and walk the three steps along to the flat that's below us. The kitchen blind is drawn, but there's a light behind it. I hold my breath. Is Brayker still awake? Is he hiding just behind the blind, waiting to pull it up and take a picture of me so he can show the police?

I don't move. I can feel my heart beating. My feet are so cold that I think my toes might freeze together. If I'm going to do it, I have to do it now.

I hold the egg in my palm like I'm weighing it, then I wiggle my hand so I can feel the insides slopping around. I lift my hand and then, smash! The egg splats on Brayker's door. The sharp edges of eggshell poke into my skin. The white dribbles down my wrist. I rub it all over the door, then turn away and run.

I open my front door slowly. Everything's still dark. I go into the bathroom and wash the egg off my arm. Some of the yolk has dripped onto my sock. I take that off and wash it too, squeezing out as much water as I can. I flush the toilet in case Plum's listening out for me like Mum does. Then I go back into my bedroom. I fold my sock across the radiator. It's not on, but it might dry a bit by morning. Mum forgot to do any washing this week and it's my last clean sock.

I get back into bed. The sheets are cold and I can't feel my feet. Venom could bite my big toe right off and I wouldn't know. I wish I could train

my rats to keep me warm. They could be furry
sleep slippers.

I close my eyes. I still can't sleep, but I don't
feel so cross now that Brayker's gonna find that
mess on his door.

Chapter 5

Plum

The next morning, Plum bangs on my door. I should have told her that I'm good at waking up. I never used to be, but Venom and Vulture need their breakfast, so I'm already filling up their bowls when Plum calls me.

I come out and it's weird that she's dressed already. Mum's normally just in her old leggings and a Queen T-shirt. That's unless she's got an appointment with her probation officer. If she doesn't go to the appointments, she'll go back to prison.

Mum's gone to every single appointment with her probation officer since she got out. She always wakes up on time and wears good clothes. She spends ages in the bathroom making her hair neat and asks me to check that the back isn't all messed up.

We wrote all the appointment dates on the calendar so we could both remember when they were. I even texted them to Gran as extra back-up. Gran would make sure Mum had the money for the bus. If Mum felt too tired, we'd make sure she still went. And she did. Yeah, there's a tick next to every appointment. But Mum still got taken away by the police yesterday.

"I've got to go to work before college," Plum says. "But I've left breakfast out for you."

Mum always tells me to help myself, but Plum's laid it out on the table. A bowl with cornflakes in it. A bottle of milk. A banana and a glass of orange juice. It's like it's my birthday.

"Put everything away when you're done," Plum says. "And wash up your bowl and stuff."

I nod.

"And make sure your rats are in their cage." Plum looks around me into the bedroom. "If they escape, you might not get them back. You understand, Al?"

I nod again.

"Right," Plum says. "I've got a careers meeting after college and then I'm back to work."

"Work?" I ask.

She laughs. "Yes, Al! It's not just you and your mum that got scammed by Dad! He doesn't give me and my mum money, neither. I'm working with a care agency. I help people who can't do stuff for themselves. See you later."

Plum races out. I sit down at the table. It's like I'm in a restaurant and a waiter's brought my food to me. I do all my washing up afterwards so the sink's empty. I even remember to put the milk back in the fridge. Did Plum notice that an egg was missing? Not unless she opened the box and I don't think she did.

I grin to myself. Brayker's gonna have a shock when he opens his door. Now I wish I'd taken two eggs and cracked one open on Brayker's doorstep. His feet would skid in it as soon as he came out.

I put on my school uniform. My sock's still a bit wet, but I'll forget about it soon. I rub the armpits of my shirt with deodorant. Now we've got money on the electricity key, I can wash everything later, especially as Gran gave us that washing powder too.

I go back into my room and tap the cage. Venom ignores me. She's too busy munching her breakfast. Vulture comes over to the bars and nibbles my finger.

"Later," I say.

I shove all my books into my bag. I haven't done any homework, so I'll have to tell Mrs Miles, my tutor, about Mum. Not everything, but just enough. I don't want no one to shout at me today in case I shout back and get excluded again. I know Mum doesn't want to have to visit the school again because of me. Especially when we both promised each other we'd be good. Or even worse, Gran would have to come to school instead of Mum.

I close my bedroom door, slip on my shoes and unhook my key. I make sure I lock the front door properly when I'm outside. I'm early. I don't have to run for the bus. I've got time to take the other stairs, the ones at the far end of the balcony instead of the ones near to us. It means I can get a good long look at Brayker's door. There should be a big eggy smear on it. If the sun's been shining on it, it might be a bit smelly too.

I get halfway along the balcony and look down at Brayker's flat. I realise that I'm licking my lips. Brayker needs to learn a lesson. He can't mess with my family and get away with it. I lean on the railing so I have a proper view of the mess.

But there isn't no mess. The door's clean. It's like it didn't happen. Like I didn't happen.

I take a big breath in and I have to stop myself running home to take out Venom and Vulture to calm me down. I don't even have to stroke them. Even if I just watch them race round and chase each other it makes me feel better. I breathe in and try to open a space in my head so I can imagine them in there. It's hard, but it's working. I turn away and carry on walking along the balcony.

Maybe Brayker did hear me last night and came out to check what happened. Or he could have cleaned it all away this morning. It doesn't mean I never did it. And the thing is, Brayker wouldn't have known it was me that did it. He needs to know it's me. I want him to know it's me. I need to do something bigger. I've got all day at school to make my plans.

Chapter 6

Ty

It's first break at school. I'm waiting to see my head of year about what Mrs Miles calls "Al's home situation" when I hear shouting. It's not just shouting. There's a load of swearing in with the shouting too. I feel myself blush, because I've shouted like that before.

Mr Seely, the deputy head, is marching towards me with a boy who looks like he must be Year 10. Mr Seely is carrying a football. The boy's pulling the biggest screwface ever. The only other time I've seen a boy look that mad is when I see myself in a mirror.

The boy's yelling about his friend who was supposed to save the goal but missed it. The boy says *he* should be here instead, because it's all his fault. Mr Seely says *that* isn't going to help the Year 8 who got hit by the ball flying into the window. It's just as well the window was open, or it could have been much worse.

Much worse. Yeah. I don't want to see no one covered in broken window glass, but, breaking a window … It gets me thinking hard.

The talk with my head of year goes OK. She checks with my social worker that it's all right for Plum to stay with me as long as it isn't for more than a couple of days and that Gran's around as back-up. My head of year says she'll have a word with my teachers too.

I sit through Religious Studies thinking about the smashing sound Brayker's kitchen window would make if it got hit by something hard. As long as no one's behind the window, why can't I …? All I need is a brick.

My plans don't normally work because there's too many bits to them. If one bit doesn't work, the other bits go wrong. I need to make my plans easier. A brick into Brayker's window is easy.

*

I take the long way back from the bus stop because I don't want to pass the shop where Mum was arrested. If I see that same security guard standing out there, I might end up shouting. That's not part of my plan. I've got to remember to keep it simple. It'll be even more simple if Mum's already come back home. I'll still want to make Brayker pay, but if Mum tells me to calm down, I will. I don't want to move again.

As I'm walking through the estate, I see a skip full of building rubble and it makes me think that my plan is meant to happen. I notice a big chunk of brick and squeeze it into my rucksack. It's really heavy. It feels like I'm carrying another person in there, but if Mum's not home when I get there, carrying the brick's gonna be worth it.

I climb the stairs along the other end of the block from our flat so I can study Brayker's kitchen window on my way along the balcony. I wonder how hard I need to throw the brick. Do I need to do a run up to make sure the brick flies proper hard and fast? Brayker's flat is on the corner, like ours, so I've got the long balcony to run along. Do I throw the brick underhand? I swing my arm back then forward. No, I have to lob it overhand to get the strength I need.

As I get closer, I see a shape behind Brayker's window. Maybe he's doing his washing up after having a massive long lunch from all the shopping he did after Mum was arrested. Or ... Brayker could be spying on me. Did he see me moving my arm like I was planning to throw something? Can he see how my bag's all sunk because it's so heavy from the brick? I put my head down and scurry along like Vulture does when she's been told off for chewing something she shouldn't.

I open our front door slowly. Of course I'm hoping that Mum's behind it and she's gonna pull it the rest of the way open, then grab me and hug me like she does when she hasn't seen me for a while. But the flat's silent. I go in and close the door behind me. Mum's not here. But I still look around, in case she's been home first and had to go out. She could have left me a note. There's nothing.

I go into my bedroom. My rats know when I'm home. They come to the front of the cage to welcome me. I close my bedroom door and take them both out. Vulture runs off and starts climbing up my duvet. Venom just sits in my hand and twitches her whiskers at me. She makes a tiny squeak, then shoots off to find her sister.

I don't understand why people don't like rats like mine. These aren't dustbin rats. They don't carry no diseases. They're no different from hamsters or gerbils, and no one gets scared about *them*.

I'm just putting Venom and Vulture back in their cage when the phone rings. Gran made us have a landline in case me and Mum run out of mobile phone credit and she can't get through to us. She says she'd rather pay for our telephone than get stressed out if she hasn't heard from us. I wish Gran would pay for WiFi too, but she says that's down to Mum. I even tried to tell her that I can't do my homework without it, but Gran thinks I should go to the library or stay behind for the school's homework club.

Gran says she's phoning to see how things are with me and Plum. I tell her they're all right even though I reckon she's spoken to Plum already. I wait. I know Gran's got more to say, but it's like she can't find the words.

"Is Plum staying longer?" I ask. "Because Mum ..."

"Well, Al ..." Gran starts, but her voice fades out like there's a bad signal.

I have to ask Gran to say it again, louder. She says the words. Mum's been taken back to prison. It was bad enough that Mum was caught stealing from the shop, but the guard is claiming she hit him.

The fiery bubbles start bumping in my head. I push my lips together tight until my teeth dig in, but it doesn't push the bubbles away. I kick the wall. It doesn't do anything to the wall, but my toe feels like I dropped the brick on it.

Brick. Yeah. I think of it smashing into glass.

I realise the phone is on the floor. I'm feeling floppy again, like I did in the shop, and I slide down the wall until I'm next to it. I pick up the phone and put it back to my ear. Gran's gone. As soon as I replace the handset, it rings again. It's Gran. She's stressed out because she thinks something's happened to me. She's gonna leave work straight away and come round. She'll even take me back to hers for the evening.

No! She can't do that! It will ruin the plan! So I do my breaths and make my voice calm. I tell Gran I dropped the phone by accident. I ask her to tell me what's gonna happen next with Mum and make sure I carry on making calm noises while she explains. Gran says we're lucky because Mum's in a prison not too far from London, so she'll arrange for us to visit her as soon as possible. She's sure Mum won't be in prison for long. She's spoken to

Mum's lawyer, who's already working hard to get Mum home soon.

That's good. I know Mum's like me and sometimes starts shouting if she's trying to say something and the other person isn't listening. A lawyer can say the things for Mum instead. It isn't like Mum was trying to steal diamonds or nothing. She just wanted to get me my tea.

When I've finished talking to Gran, I sit there. I always had these pictures in my head of how it was going to be when me and Mum were back together for good. I never thought we were ever going to be rich, even if I wish we were. But we'd be more like other kids and their mums. Mum would be here when I come home from school. Every time. Or come to parents' evenings at school and know some of the other mums and chat to them.

Being here together could have been the best thing that's happened to us so far. Like I said before, nothing in this place is special, but it's about us being together. Just us. Most evenings, we sit around watching TV together. We plan what we're gonna watch beforehand so we don't have no arguments. At Lee and Macey's, I always got sent to bed at 8 p.m. with my phone taken away. Gran would only let me watch one hour of TV, *and* she decided what I could watch.

Now Mum's back in a tiny prison cell. I don't even know if she's got a TV. If she did and I knew what she was watching, I'd try to watch the same thing, like we were together at home again.

It's getting dark. My bum hurts from the hard floor and my legs have gone to sleep. I'm hungry, but I ignore it. I want to carry out my plan before Plum comes home. She said she's gonna be late, so I've got time. If the police take me away, Plum won't be blamed.

I make myself stand up. I feel like I'm made from rusty iron. I find my rucksack and bring it back to the hallway. I unzip it and take out the brick. It's more like half a brick with cement stuck to it. Some of it's flaked all over the books in my bag. But it doesn't matter. My teachers have been told to go easy on me.

I find an old French worksheet squashed in the back of an exercise book. I take a pen from inside my bag and write Plum a note. I ask her if she'll keep Venom and Vulture safe for me if I get taken to the police station. I explain how to feed my rats and to make sure she changes their water. They've got plenty of room to run around in the cage, but they do like to chase each other round my room. If they don't come back when she calls them, she can use some sweetcorn as bait. They love it.

My eyes are prickling. I don't want to leave my rats. They're my best friends. I've moved around so much I haven't had time to make any other ones. But I have to do this, for Mum.

I run my hand over the brick. There's a sharp edge under the cement. Maybe I don't even have to throw the brick. I can just smash it into the window while I'm still holding it. That would work.

Light suddenly shines into the glass panel above our front door. The lights in the whole block have come on. It's getting late. I pick up the brick, open the door and peer out. Good. No one's about. I don't want someone realising my plan and trying to stop me. I shove my door keys in my pocket and close the door after me.

I walk down the stairs holding the brick behind my back. I turn the corner. Brayker's blind is down in the window, but I can see light between the gaps. There's a shadow too. I jerk myself back. I can't smash the glass if someone's standing there. I have to wait until they leave the kitchen. I don't even have to check Brayker's window. I can see the light reflected on the ground below.

The brick's starting to feel heavy, but I don't want to put it down. I'm hungry and it's getting a bit colder too. I think about leaving the brick on the floor and going back upstairs. There's proper food in the fridge waiting for me. As I rub my stomach, the ground in front of Brayker's kitchen window goes dark. The kitchen is empty. I grip my brick and step forward.

"Not a good idea," a voice says.

I jump and drop the brick. It thumps down about a centimetre away from my big toe. A face is peering out from under a dark hood. The man is behind me, on the corner of the balcony. He isn't much taller than me, but I think he's a lot older. His coat is buttoned from the bottom right up to the very top, so his neck stretches out like an ostrich.

"What do you mean?" I say.

The man points at the brick and replies, "Don't take me for a mug, right?"

I can't think of nothing to say back. He's come up behind me and seen me with the brick in my hand, peering round at Brayker's. I shrug.

He says, "We've got a stew on if you want some, Al."

I frown. Stew? And ... "How do you know my name?" I ask.

"I saw your mum soon after you moved in," the man explains. "We had a quick chat. I let her know that we were here if you needed anything. I'm Ty by the way."

Ty flips down his hood. He's got long dark hair with grey bits that stand up at the front and a row of silver rings in each of his ears. There's a stud in his nose too. Ty holds out his hand for me to shake. There's a ring like a skull on one finger and another that I can't make out ... It's hard to see in the light.

"It's a rat," Ty says. "In memory of my pet, Scabies. May he rest in peace. A lot of people don't like rats."

"I do," I say. "I love them."

"Another rat lover!" Ty smiles and I shake his hand. "It takes one to know one! So how about that stew?"

There's food upstairs in the fridge, more food than normal. But stew sounds so good, maybe with a pile of mashed potatoes. I look at Ty. He may have talked to Mum, but I've never met him before. My brain's yelling at me, saying I shouldn't go into a stranger's flat, even if Ty does like rats. But my stomach's yelling harder. Stew! And I won't be eating by myself.

I run after Ty. I look back at Brayker's flat. The blind's been pulled up and I think I see the shape of a face in the darkness behind the window, but maybe it was just a shadow from the balcony lights.

*

Ty lives in one of the flats halfway down the long balcony. We stand outside while he fishes for his keys in a pocket. The small window in the kitchen is open and the stew smells are creeping out to me.

"Careful," Ty says. "We're a bit crowded in here."

He opens the door and I almost trip over a stack of boxes in the hallway.

"Are you moving out?" I ask him.

"Nah." He points to an open door. "In here."

I'm lucky that I'm pretty thin, so I can fit round the boxes and into the sitting room. Another guy's on the sofa watching *Countdown* on a TV that's bigger than our fridge. The sofa's big and kind of baggy like it ate too much and fell asleep. The guy's feet are resting on a plastic box that looks like it's full of tools.

There's stuff everywhere. A small table is so crammed with things I can hardly see the glass it's made from. There's shells that look like giant snails lived in them, a load of different size candle holders, books, magazines, a mug from Prince William's wedding, an alarm clock and loads of things that I can't work out. The room is painted white, like ours, except for a corner behind the TV that's been covered in wallpaper with silver circles on it. Paintings, photographs, an old map and a big gold mirror hang on the walls.

"This is Pete," Ty says. "Pete, meet Al. He's a fellow rat-lover! But I caught him getting ready to lob a brick into Noah Brayker's window."

"I wouldn't do that!" Pete says. "Even if he is a bit of a misery. What's he done to you?"

I don't know if Mum told Ty she's been in prison. Gran says I shouldn't mention it unless I have to, because it might make people think bad things about us.

"He was horrible to my mum," I say.

Pete shakes his head and says, "Like I said, Noah's a misery but that's still not a good reason to bust his window." He turns back to the TV. "Ty!

I can get a seven-letter word out of that! Just give me time and—"

Ty grabs the remote off the sofa arm and pauses the programme. "Of course you can," Ty says. "You've seen this one twice already."

Pete gets up. He looks a bit older than Ty, maybe nearer Gran's age. His hair's been cut really short and his eyebrows stick out. He's wearing a shirt with a waistcoat, like Farmer Boggis in *Fantastic Mr Fox*. His trousers are baggy, like the sofa.

When Pete looks at me, his eyes are bright blue. "I used to think that I'd be clever enough to go on a TV show like that," he says, "but ..." He shakes his head.

Pete slides past the table and us. I think he's so used to having stuff everywhere he doesn't notice it.

Ty must have seen me looking around.

"Some of it's for sale," Ty says. "Some of it's for giving away."

"Where do you get it all from?" I ask.

"Skips. The stuff people throw away. Good stuff. Loads of it not even used."

"Come and get it!" That's Pete calling from the kitchen. My stomach rumbles so hard I think it's gonna walk me to the kitchen itself.

The kitchen is tiny, with room for only one person at a time. They've just got one fridge, but there's two kettles and more boxes stacked up beside a wall. A wooden shelf is full of saucepans – one of them's so big you could wash a baby in it.

But the pans on the cooker are more interesting. Pete's already spooned mashed potato onto three plates. He's adding some peas. I hate peas, but I don't want to tell him. If I mix them with the stew, I won't be able to taste them.

Last comes the stew. My stomach twangs like it's smiling. The food smells like when you crack open a warm pasty and the steam wafts the flavours up your nose. Gran used to buy me a pasty when she picked me up from my old school on Wednesdays. I'd count to ten before I took a bite, because that would make it taste way better. This stew, it's like all those times I've counted to ten joined together. It's gonna taste like a million.

At last Pete hands me a tray with my plate of food and a fork.

"Take it into the sitting room, Al," Pete says. "Make yourself comfortable."

I wind my way past the boxes in the hallway and the small table and the plastic box of tools and I sit down at the far end of the sofa. It's time. Time to taste the stew. And, yeah, it tastes like a million and more.

We eat and watch telly with our plates on our laps. Gran would go mad if she knew I wasn't sitting at a table. That makes the stew taste even better. When I've finished, Pete gives me a second helping, then some apple tart.

Afterwards, I could have dropped asleep right there on the sofa, but I notice the time on the alarm clock. I want to ignore it because I'm so comfortable, but Plum might be back by now. And she'll have read my note and thought ...

She probably thinks I've run away. What if she's called the police?

I jump up. "I'm really sorry, I have to go," I say. "My sister will be worried."

"Your sister?" Ty asks.

"Plum. She's ... um ... staying with me."

"She's staying with you now?" Ty says.

"That makes sense," Pete says.

"What does?" I ask. I'm feeling confused now. How do they know Plum? Pete doesn't answer. His mouth's moving as he's trying to work out a word puzzle on the TV again.

Ty's been sitting on the arm of the sofa. He goes off into the hallway and I hear boxes being moved about. I wriggle free from the sitting room and follow him. Ty hands me a box.

"A smoothie maker. Me and Pete have already got two of 'em. Give it to Plum. She might forgive you."

I nod. "Do you know Plum?" I ask.

"I've seen her about," Ty says.

Plum has only been here a day, but Ty seems pretty good at keeping an eye out for people.

"I'll just drop this stew off," Pete says. He's behind Ty holding a tray and a bowl with a tea towel over it.

"Where's that one going?" Ty asks.

"To Mrs Vera," Pete replies. "I saw her in the shop this morning and she's been feeling low. This might cheer her up a bit."

Pete opens the front door and there's Plum on the doorstep. Her hand's in the air like she's just about to knock. She steps back.

"I've come to take you home," Plum says to me. "I don't want you outstaying your welcome."

"How did you know I was here?" I ask.

Plum taps her nose. "Walls have eyes."

So everyone in the block is spying on me? I look up at the rows of windows. I can't see no one.

We head home. I feel warm and full. I try not to look at Brayker's flat just in case I start to feel cross again. While Plum walks ahead, I pick up the brick and drop it in the chute. It rattles down and thumps into the garbage below.

I round the corner to our flat and see the lights are on. It makes it feel friendly.

Plum's waiting in the kitchen. She points at the box I'm holding. "What's that you've got?"

I hold it out. "It's from Ty," I say. "For you."

Plum opens it and her eyes go wide. "I've wanted one of these for ages!"

"Ty gets all this stuff from skips."

She nods. "Yes."

I frown. It's like she knows already.

Plum smiles and says, "Thank you for this! Well, thank Ty. I'm going to test it out."

I go into the bedroom. My note to Plum is right where I left it. I crumple it up and throw it under my bed. I drag off my duvet and wrap it round me like I'm a hot dog. I lie down on the floor next to the cage and close my eyes.

Chapter 7

Pete

It's been a couple of weeks since Mum was arrested. Plum and me are getting on OK. Even Blessing agreed that we're all right for now, but Plum has to let her know if there's any problems. I think Blessing means if *I'm* a problem.

Gran's popped round twice to make sure I've got food and clean clothes, and she talks to Plum every day. Gran's been to see Mum and she says Mum wants to see me too. But no one's asked me if I want to see her. I *do*, but here. Right here. Not in a prison. But I don't want Mum to think I don't care about her, so I said I will go.

I've been to Ty and Pete's twice more as well and there was different stuff piled everywhere. Last time there were bits of a washing machine spread over the table in the sitting room. Pete said they had to be gone by that night. I'd asked Ty if he always got rid of everything. He laughed and said most folk in the block were happy when he knocked at their door. Sometimes they put in requests. Except Noah Brayker.

"He won't take nothing unless I can swear it hasn't been touched by one of our friends," Ty told me, stroking his rat ring. "Mr Brayker has a bit of a fear of Rattus rattus."

I smiled, knowing that this was the Latin name for black rats. "But you haven't got any pet rats now," I said. "So they're not gonna touch nothing."

"But you know what they say about London," Pete said. "You're never more than six feet away from a rat. A couple of years ago, the pest people found a rat's nest in the bins. It was a nasty, nasty business and I don't think Brayker ever recovered."

Good. I want him to feel bad.

That last time I was there Pete had cooked a curry. I didn't think I liked curry, but this was different from school curry. The other time we had baked potato with cheese and ham. That's my favourite meal. But Pete said that the best day was Sunday, when he did a roast dinner.

Roast dinner! Gran used to make them, but I was always being told about my manners, so they

stopped tasting good. Pete says he does everything.
Potatoes, Yorkshire puddings, gravy – everything. I
touch my stomach as I think about it.

So today I'm going to Pete and Ty's for Sunday
lunch. Plum doesn't mind. She even walks me to
their door and says, "Hello." Ty tries to get Plum to
stay, but she says she's got a whole stack of essays
to write and some revision for a test next week.
I've got loads of work to do for school too, but I
know it's gonna be easier if my stomach's full.

Pete told me before that it wasn't just me that
was invited. He said he normally had a full house
on Sundays. I didn't think the flat could be even
more jammed up than usual, but somehow it is.
Ty must have moved some of the boxes into the
bedroom. Now there are giant beanbags in the
hallway instead and a couple of kids are sitting on
them eating bowls of ice cream. I'm scared I've
missed the roast dinner, but I spot a tray of roast
potatoes in the kitchen and smell the gravy.

"Don't be shy," Ty says.

I go into the sitting room. Three people are
crammed on the sofa. One's a woman who looks
like she could be the kids' mum. Squashed next to
her is a girl about Plum's age. She looks at me and
smiles, then carries on watching the telly. The old

man sat next to her seems to be asleep until the plates are plonked down on the table. (Yeah, even the small table's been cleared and covered in a cloth.)

Pete and Ty bring in all the food. There's even a silver cover over the meat like the ones they have in posh places on TV. The old man dives in first and fills a plate. He hands it to the woman at the end of the sofa. She says, "Thank you." He smiles and nods but doesn't say nothing. The next plate goes to the girl in the middle of the sofa. Then the old man looks at me and waves his hand at the food.

"Help yourself," the girl says. "He doesn't know what you like."

I want to ask if the man can't speak at all or if he just doesn't speak English. Maybe he can, but he's decided he doesn't want to speak. Nobody seems to mind.

I fill up my plate with chicken and potatoes and gravy and two small pieces of carrot, even though no one's checking to make sure I take vegetables. The TV stays on and we just eat and watch. I think that this is what I'm going to do every Sunday. When everyone's finished, I collect their plates and take them into the kitchen.

Pete's in there, sorting out more plates of food.
"Time for the delivery service," he says.

Ty comes in and asks, "Shall I drop off Noah
Brayker's first?"

What? I look at Ty, then Pete, then the food.
My big roast dinner does a little bounce in my
stomach. "You take him food?" I ask.

Pete sort of sighs and turns to look at me
as he says, "Of course! Everyone's welcome at
Pete's Diner. And if you can't eat in or collect, we
deliver."

"But he's horrible!" I say. "It's his fault my
mum's in prison."

Ty and Pete look at me at the same time. "In
prison?" Pete says.

I blush and feel my face growing hot. "He ... he
made the security guard think we'd been stealing
from a shop and then ..."

I remember the security guard slumped by the
fridge rubbing his head.

"My mum was in prison before," I say in a low
voice. "Now she has to go back. It's all Brayker's
fault."

Pete hands Ty a tray with some dishes. There's
tea cloths over them like before. "Don't judge

Noah, Al," Pete says. "I agree, he isn't the most friendly chap, but you don't know—"

Pete doesn't finish. Or maybe he does. I don't know because I run out of the flat. I wish I'd left the brick by the chute so I could bang it on Brayker's window as I go past. There's a bag of rubbish leaning by the wall, too fat to fit in the chute. I kick it and it explodes everywhere – lolly wrappers and drink cartons and stringy old bacon. I hope the wind blows all the nasty gooey things out so they stick to Brayker's door.

I run up the stairs and into the flat. Mum's bedroom door's closed. Plum must be in there working. Everything's quiet. No one knows I'm here. When I go into my room, even Venom and Vulture are asleep.

Chapter 8

Not Mum

It's Tuesday and this is what I've worked out:

1. I don't need roast dinner.

2. I don't need baked potato with cheese and
    ham.

3. I don't need ice cream nor apple pie.

4. I don't need Ty or Pete. I thought they
    were my friends, but they can't be. Not if
    they're friends with the person who ruined
    my life – and Mum's too. I shouldn't have
    let Ty stop me smashing Brayker's window.

My rats know how angry I am. Most people don't know that rats understand feelings. Every time I pick up Venom she tries to jump out of my hand. I've got to hold her over the bed in case she tumbles onto the floor and breaks a bone. Vulture just hides in her cage. I manage to catch her and cuddle her under my jumper, but she won't stop trembling, so I put her back.

Plum's getting fed up with me. I know because she's told me. She asked me what's wrong and I tried to explain about Pete and Ty being friends with Brayker, but she got even crosser. Plum said I had no right to sulk and Pete and Ty didn't have to ask my permission about who they wanted to help.

So I've stopped talking to anyone. What's the point? Mrs Miles, my tutor, is cross too. I don't answer in class, not even when she calls my name for the register. If a teacher wants me to answer a question, I pretend I don't hear them. If they ask me to leave the classroom, I just get up and go and don't say nothing.

Mrs Miles calls Gran in to school to talk about me. Afterwards, Gran takes me back to her place. We sit down on the sofa and I think I'm going to get another lecture, but Gran says she understands how I feel. She's worried about Mum every second of every day and knows that I am too. Mum's cross with herself for ending up back in prison and sorry that she's let me down. Gran's organised a prison visit for us so we can all talk about it. She's even got special permission from the school for me to go, but I have to promise that my behaviour will improve.

I want to promise, but I can't. It's wrong to make promises you can't keep. The last time I went to see Mum in prison, all the chairs and tables in the visiting hall were crowded together so close you could never talk about your secrets without someone else hearing. I'd still tried to tell Mum how I was feeling, but she didn't want to talk when anyone could listen in. I was sent over to a play area that was meant for little kids and sat there watching Gran hold Mum's hand.

But I do want to see Mum. I want her to know I'm on her side. And I'm still gonna make sure Brayker pays for putting her in there.

*

The night before we go and see Mum, Gran goes through her list of Things To Remember. She reminds me that I've got to dress properly, because she doesn't want any of the other visitors looking down on us. I have to wear my school shoes instead of trainers. Gran says it doesn't matter if they pinch; I just have to put up with it.

I'm not allowed to chew gum in case I forget to throw it away and take it into the prison. It's not allowed. Gran wants me to check my pockets in case I've got any Blu-Tac. That's not allowed neither.

Gran says I'm allowed to kiss my mum when I see her, but I'm not sure if I want to. Gran will have the cash for snacks – just ten quid for the three of us. Mum can have my share for chocolate. I can buy more when I come out. Gran's also got my passport. She got me one when I was ten, as she was gonna take me to EuroDisney. It never happened because Mum went to prison and it didn't seem right. But Gran says that one day we will use it properly and all go on holiday. I'm not sure if even Gran believes that.

Gran drives us to the prison. She says it's too much hassle to take a bus and a train and another bus. I hope she doesn't want to keep talking to me in the car, as I'm trying to plan what to say to Mum. I'm wearing my favourite sweatshirt for luck. I imagine Venom and Vulture sitting inside it. Their warm bodies and little squeaks would stop me feeling so sick.

There's not many spaces left in the prison car park. We have to leave the car a long way from the visitors' entrance. It's a sunny day and the sky's full of small clouds. I wonder if Mum can see them from her cell. I gulp hard. Mum's in a cell. I imagine her lying on her bed trying to look out of the window, but the bars are in the way. I try to get out of the car, but I can't breathe. Gran pats my back and waits until I'm ready.

"It's OK, Al," she says.

We walk past all the rows of cars to the reception. We wait in line. There are quite a few people ahead of us. We have to show our passports and have our photos and fingerprints taken.

"Sorry," the security guard says. "You can't wear that."

The guard's looking at me. I don't understand until she points at a sign with a list of things I'm not allowed to wear. I'm not wearing a football shirt and my top hasn't got nothing rude written on it.

Gran shakes her head, then touches my arm. "Nothing frayed or torn," she says.

My cuffs are all tatty from when Venom had a go at them.

"I should have noticed, Al," Gran says. "Are you decent underneath?"

I take off the sweatshirt. I'm wearing a plain black T-shirt.

"It could do with ironing," Gran sighs.

"Don't worry, love," the guard says to me. "You look fine."

We stash my sweatshirt in a locker and they let us into the waiting room. We find the last two seats next to each other. There's a little kid running up and down singing "The Wheels On The Bus". She keeps stopping and doing a dance when she gets to "all day long". I wish I was her and didn't know what's coming next. Gran gets a cup of tea from a vending machine, but I don't see her drinking none of it. I didn't want one. I feel so stressed I know I won't be able to swallow.

At last we're allowed to line up and go in to see Mum. Gran puts down her cup. It's still full. We get patted down by guards and go through a metal detector before we can enter the visiting hall. This one's smaller than the one we saw Mum in last time. We have to sit down first and then they'll bring Mum in.

I look around. This prison's got a play area.
There's big sheets of paper and pots of crayons and
a giant Connect Four. A lady's waiting to help the
little kids find stuff they like. She gives me a smile.
I try to smile back, but my face feels stuck.

I keep my eyes on the tea bar instead. I
wonder if I should go and get in line now so we
already have snacks when Mum comes in. I ask
Gran, but she says that it's best to wait so Mum
can choose what she wants.

The prisoners are coming in now. I try not to
stare, but I can't help it. I think they're going to
look different, maybe because they're in prison. I
should know by now that they don't. Lots of them
are thin, like Mum, but not all of them. Some
of them are older than Mum and a few look like
they're not much older than Plum. There's even
a woman who looks a bit like Gran. I want to tell
Gran, but she's twisted round watching them too.

"Trust your mum," Gran laughs. "She's always
last."

The little kid who was singing "The Wheels On
The Bus" runs past me towards the play area. One
of the prison women who's just come in catches
up with her and bends down to kiss her. I suppose
she's the kid's mum. But the kid's not interested

and starts crying. She just wants to play. The lady by the play area says something and the kid and her mum head over to a table and spread out a big roll of paper. Then they empty out a bucket of crayons. The kid looks really interested now and she and her mum start drawing together.

My mum's not here yet.

The prison officers are still bringing people in, but now most of the tables are full up.

Gran's leg is shaking like it wants to run off by itself. One more woman comes in and then there's no more. There's still a Mum-space waiting at our table. Then, there she is! Mum! Well, it looks like Mum. Same face, same hair and I've seen her in those clothes at home. But she sees us and her face doesn't change. She doesn't smile or walk faster or wave.

I realise both me and Gran are leaning forward towards Mum. Gran stands up and calls her name. Mum gives a tiny nod and comes over.

I've grown out of hugging. I've been telling Gran that for ages. I'm not little no more and I don't want no one getting close to me like that. Except Mum. I really want her to hug me, but she sits down in the chair we saved for her. She perches on the edge, like she's not planning to spend much time there. Then she smiles and I smile back. I think she's gonna say something to me, but Gran says, "Have you seen the doctor yet, Ramona?"

Mum nods.

"And?" Gran asks.

Mum doesn't say nothing.

"Are you talking to anyone?" Gran goes on. "A counsellor or someone? Have they checked your pills?"

Mum starts crying. It's like she doesn't even realise she's doing it. She doesn't make any crying sounds or wipe her face.

"Oh, Ramona!" Gran says to Mum.

Gran has tissues in her hand and wipes Mum's face. Mum still doesn't move or say nothing. Gran's lips are pushed into a line and her chin is trembling. She blinks hard and takes a deep breath.

"Al, would you like to get us some drinks and snacks?" Gran asks me.

I look at the massive queue, then back at Mum.

"What do you want, Mum?" I ask.

Gran hands me some fifty pence coins. They feel warm and a bit damp and I hold them so tight the edges press into my palm.

"Why don't you decide?" Gran says in a whisper.

I look at Mum again, but she's still crying. I stand up and go and join the end of the queue. There's only two people serving at the counter and they're not very fast. There are more kids in the play area now. There's crayons spread out all over the long table and crumpled-up paper and pipe cleaners. One of the women from the prison is sitting on a beanbag with her kid on her lap, reading him a story. It's like they're somewhere else. Not here.

I look back at our table. Gran is leaning towards Mum and holding her hand. They're still like that when I get back with bottles of Coke, a Kit Kat and a muffin.

"Thanks, Al," Mum says.

And she smiles again. It hurts inside me, because this is a real Mum smile. I've got a gallery of real Mum smiles in my head. Whenever she breaks her promises, I think about those smiles because of what she always says afterwards. It's the one thing that I know for sure Mum means.

"I love you, Al," she says.

"I know," I say really quietly.

Gran sniffs.

"I'm really sorry," Mum says. "I shouldn't have … This is my fault. I shouldn't have gone to the shop. I should have listened to you."

I shake my head hard. "It's not your fault!" I say. "It's mine! If I hadn't followed you, you'd have been all right."

"No, Al." Mum's crying again. Her nose is red and the dark patches under her eyes look even darker. "I'm your parent. I should know better."

"You just wanted to make sure we had something to eat," I say. "If Brayker hadn't …"

My anger is bubbling again. It's not just small bubbles inside my head now but a giant bubble and I'm trapped inside it. Gran touches my arm.

"It's OK, Al," Gran says.

"It's not," I say. I know I'm too loud. My voice won't get lower. "This isn't Mum's fault! It's because of me and Brayker!"

"Al!" Gran's voice is sharp. "Sit down!"

I hadn't realised I'd stood up. I sit down again and make myself take deep breaths.

"Is there anything I can do to help?" A woman is standing behind Mum. She's wearing a bright blue T-shirt with "Family Friends" written on it.

Mum says, "I would like to go back, please."

Gran makes a noise that sounds like "no". I just look at Mum.

"Sorry, Mum," I say. "Please don't go. Please!" I touch her arm. "I promise I won't say anything else. I promise!"

Mum sighs. "I shouldn't have asked you to come, Al. Being here makes me ... It's like I'm at the bottom of a deep hole. I don't want to pull you down with me, Al."

The Family Friends woman calls over one of the prison guards. Mum kisses me on the forehead and then Gran. Gran's still holding Mum's hand and it looks like she's not gonna let it go. Then she does. And Mum walks away. The Family Friends woman gives Gran her card and tells her to get in touch if we want to talk.

We're taken back out to the reception. The car's so far away it feels like we're walking home.

Chapter 9

Fargo

Gran wants me to stay with her for the night, but who's gonna look after Venom and Vulture? She finally agrees to take me home. The main door opens as Gran's parking outside the block. Brayker comes out wheeling a shopping trolley. My anger starts bubbling again. It's his fault Mum's stuck there in that place.

I take a deep breath and when I get into the flat, I go straight to my bedroom. Plum tries to talk to me, but I close the door behind me. I can still hear her talking to Gran in the hall.

"It was a hard day for him," Gran says. "Keep an eye on Al for me, will you?"

It was a hard day for Gran too. I didn't let her know that I saw her crying on the way back to the car.

When Gran leaves, I open the cage and take my rats out, put them on the bed and lie down. Vulture jumps off the bed again and goes charging round the bedroom. Venom stays with me. I take off my sweatshirt and make it into a nest. Venom buries herself in the hood and after a while Vulture comes and joins her. I wrap my arms round both of them and close my eyes.

I don't go to sleep. The pictures in my head are too bright. I see Mum in her cell. Maybe she's lying on her bed, just like me, but she doesn't have Venom and Vulture to keep her company. Mum's crying. Then I see Brayker and he's smiling. I open my eyes and shake my head to try to get rid of him. But he'll always be there until I make him understand that he can't get away with what he's done to us.

Plum knocks on my door. She says Ty's brought some stew for me. I pretend I'm asleep and don't answer. I'm never gonna eat his food again.

*

It's been two days now since we went to see Mum. Plum made me some porridge this morning with loads of golden syrup on top before she rushed out. I eat my breakfast really slowly. Then I wash my bowl really slowly. I pick my blazer up and head to the bus stop.

I wait ages for the right bus. Halfway to school, the driver announces that the bus is gonna end its journey before it's supposed to. We all have to get off and wait for another bus. I don't want to wait.

There's a park across the road and I go over and sit on a bench by the pond. I was late for school yesterday too. Then I got sent to the deputy head because I wouldn't open my Maths book. What's the point? I don't understand any of it anyway. Mr Seely called Gran while I was in his office. Gran was at work. He let her speak to me. She was furious and couldn't come and collect me. She said she'd have more to say later.

But it wasn't Gran who called me later. It was my dad. The dad who left me and Mum before I can remember because he was in love with someone else. (Plum says I don't have a right to be cross with Dad because he left Plum's mum for mine.) I didn't want to speak to him, but Plum passed me her phone without telling me who it was.

"Hello, son," Dad said.

I reckon he called me that because he can't remember my name. Plum was giving me laser eyes, so I made my mouth say "Hello" back. Dad started going on about me needing my education and how I have to focus at school so I don't end up like him. He was still talking when I gave the phone back to Plum and went into my room. I haven't seen Dad since he brought around a birthday present three years ago. He never gives Mum money for me. He won't even help with buying my school uniform. He's just one big wasteman.

As I sit on the bench now in the park I hear someone calling, "Fargo! Come back!"

A dog's running among the tall grass. It's one of them big furry dogs, like a husky. Then I see a kid, frozen stiff, standing right in the dog's path. The kid's only small, maybe Year 1, and she can't move. I don't know if I should do something. She's with a man who could be her dad, but he's just staring at the dog, frozen too.

"Fargo!" the owner calls. I can see her now. She's about the same age as Mum and looking really stressed.

Suddenly, the kid starts screaming. It's the way people scream when they're surrounded by zombies in films. It's the sort of screaming that makes you think their throat's gonna explode. The dad grabs the little girl and lifts her into his arms just as the dog reaches them. Fargo slows down, then runs straight past like they're just not there. The owner's still chasing after the dog, waving her lead.

I can see the dad whispering in the little girl's ear. She's stopped screaming, but her whole body is moving like the screams are still inside her and can't get out. Her dad rubs her back and kisses her forehead, but it doesn't make a difference. He starts walking towards the park exit, still carrying her. Man, it looks like that little girl's never gonna stop being scared.

Some people are as scared of rats as that little girl was scared of the dog. I mean, I've seen it. When I was in the last foster home, one of Maya's school friends came round. But she only stayed a few minutes. She went into Maya's room, saw Venom and Vulture and ran out crying, all the way into the street. She wouldn't even come back into the house.

And now I'm thinking.

And now I'm smiling.

Because ... I know someone else who's supposed to be terrified of rats. Someone who needs to be taught a lesson.

I walk home, not too fast because I want to work this out in my head. I need a good plan. One that's simple and gonna work without me losing Venom and Vulture. I need to be careful.

I walk up the stairs to our flat like I'm a spy, looking round the corner in case anyone sees me. I don't want no one reporting me for being home from school. Not now I know what I'm gonna do.

I let myself in. My heart's beating so hard it's making my chest hurt. I go into the kitchen first. Plum's left me a note. It's stuck to the fridge with the magnet shaped like a banana. It says that she's working this afternoon, but she shouldn't be back too late. I've got enough time.

First, I need a box. I remember that Mum kept the box from my school shoes in case I needed to take them back. I check behind the sofa. Yeah, it's there. Perfect. I make some holes in the lid and take it into my room. I drop some hay into the bottom of it. I close my bedroom door and open Venom and Vulture's cage. I scoop out Venom first. She looks at me and twitches her whiskers. I kiss the top of her head.

"You're the sensible one," I say to Venom. "All you have to do is poke your head over the top of the box when I take off the lid. Don't do nothing more."

Because that's all I need if Brayker hates rats as much as Ty said he does. I want to make Brayker feel as scared as I am. Scared that Mum's not gonna stop being sad. Scared that she's gonna come out of prison and go back to her bad friends. Scared that I'm gonna move again and again and I'll never have a real home.

I take Vulture out of the cage and kiss her too. She's the naughty one.

"You heard what I said to your sister," I say. "It's the same for you, but maybe you can make a face and squeak really loud, yeah?"

I bend over and Vulture headbutts my nose. I kiss them both again, then carefully drop them into the box. I put the lid on and hold it down. They scrabble around inside. I drop the tea towel over the top. It's really thin so I know air can get through, but I'm still worried. I don't want my rats to be in there too long. If they both do too much weeing, it's going to make the box soggy and they might fall through the bottom.

I hold the box up towards my face.

"When you hear me say 'you better say sorry', I'm going to open the lid," I explain. "It's just going to be for a few seconds, but that should be enough."

I think I hear Venom squeak.

"Are you ready?" I ask.

Because I am. I'm really ready. I can even hear Brayker's shaky voice in my head begging me to take my rats away.

I hold the lid clamped shut and try to move gently so Venom and Vulture don't get too shaken. I make sure my key is in my pocket and slowly leave our flat. I have to hook the door closed with my foot so I can hold the box tight.

I go down the stairs carefully, like I'm holding a tray with a hundred glasses on it. I turn the corner. Just three steps are going to take me up to Brayker's door. Step one. My heart sounds like it's marching up and down inside me. Step two. I can hear noises from inside the box. Venom and Vulture are whispering to each other. I hope they're not planning no bad behaviour. Step three. *Brayker, it's time for payback!*

I knock on the door as hard as I can. I hold up the box with the tea towel over it so if Brayker looks out of the kitchen window, he's gonna think I've come from Ty and Pete's with a bowl of food.

There's a sound behind the door. It's a latch being pulled back.

Brayker! This is for my mum! I think.

The door opens.

Huh?

This isn't right! No, this really isn't right. I forget to hold the box and it drops onto the doorstep. The lid flies off and Venom and Vulture leap out and away into the flat.

Chapter 10

Laurie

It's Plum. The person who's opened the door is Plum and she looks mad. She swears and races back inside the flat. I just stand there for a second and my head's bursting with questions. Then I go in, close the front door and follow her.

"What are you doing here?" I yell.

Plum turns round. "I could ask you the same thing! I seriously can't believe you've done this!"

"But you're not supposed to be here!" I reply.

"And you are, Al?" Plum says, and swears. "Where have your rats got to? We need to find them straight away, before Mr Brayker comes home. He seriously hates them."

I open my mouth to tell Plum I know that, but she says, "Don't even think of giving me any backchat right now!" Her voice turns into a

whisper. "Seriously don't, Al! You need to find
your furry friends and take them home. Right.
Away."

"But—" I begin, but Plum cuts me off.

"Or I'm going to call the council and tell them
there's a pest problem. And you know what the
council do to rats, don't you?"

I nod.

"Good. So start in there!" Plum nods towards
the kitchen. "I think that's where they went."

Brayker's flat is like ours, with the rooms in
the same place. There's a sound coming from
the sitting room, like laughing but not normal
laughing. It's like when you've been running really
hard and then you think of something funny and
the laugh can't come out properly because your
breath hurts.

"I'll be back in a minute," Plum says. She goes
into the sitting room and closes the door.

Brayker's kitchen is painted dark grey. There's
a table pushed against the wall and it's got a stack
of tins on it. They're all the same. Tomato soup.
There's some pictures on the wall above the table.
They're all old black and white ones. I move closer
to see the pictures better. One of them looks like a

photo of Brayker, but he's much younger. It's weird to think he was young.

Then I hear a scuffling noise. It's coming from beneath the cooker. One of my rats must be under there.

"Venom!" I say in my singing voice. "Vulture."

I lie on the floor and turn my head sideways to try to see them, but I can't. I shove my hand under the cooker and wiggle it. I don't know why. Maybe she'll recognise my fingers and come out.

She doesn't. My rats aren't good at doing what they're told unless they have treats. I need some treats! Vulture likes Coco Pops, because that's how she first got trained. But chocolate isn't so good for her. Sweetcorn's good, but I don't have any, not even at home. Maybe Brayker's got something I can use. He's probably got so much food he won't notice nothing missing.

I stand up and brush myself down. My cheek's all cold from the floor and I rub it warm again. Brayker's fridge is smaller than ours and looks even older. I yank it open. The door rattles, like it's got loads of beer or Coke inside. And yeah, the fridge *is* full up. But it doesn't look like food. The bottles have got labels on them. It's medicine. There are some eggs and some bacon and a bowl of beans and a tub that looks like it's got some of the tomato soup in it. But everything else is medicine.

Is Brayker really ill? Is that what makes him so cross?

I didn't make him ill. Anyway, Mum's not well, but Brayker doesn't care. Why should I care about him?

There's a small bowl of grapes right at the back of the fridge. Venom loves grapes. They're special treats because we only get them when Gran buys them for us. I take a grape out of the bowl. It's soft, like it's going to burst everywhere if I squeeze it too hard.

I kneel down by the cooker.

"Venom!" I sing her name again. I hear more scuffling. I stretch out my hand and offer the grape. "Come on."

I feel whiskers tickle my fingers, then a slight pull at the grape. I draw my hand back and wait. First a nose and then whisker tips appear from under the cooker. Yeah, it's Venom.

"Nice juicy grape," I say. I give it a really tiny squeeze to make sure Venom gets the scent. "Don't you want it?"

She flattens herself down so she can get out, then pops herself up again so it looks like she could never have fitted under there in the first place. I pick Venom up with one hand and give her the grape with the other. She holds it in her tiny hands and nibbles at it quickly until there's nothing left.

"Good girl," I say and kiss her head. It smells of old food.

The kitchen door slams open. Venom jerks and tries to jump out of my arms. I just manage to hold on to her.

Plum closes the door and leans on it. "Mr Brayker is going to be home any minute, Al."

"You scared Venom!" I say.

"Just like you were trying to scare Mr Brayker, right?"

I hold Venom closer but don't say nothing.

"Go upstairs and put Venom in her cage and come right back," Plum tells me.

I lift up my jumper and snuggle Venom underneath. She clings on to my T-shirt. Rats' hearts beat more than four times faster than humans. I wonder if Venom can feel mine. She wouldn't know what it was.

I go back upstairs to our flat and take Venom into my room. I put her in her cage and make sure she's got water and food. I definitely need to clean it out later. It's not smelling so good. Venom stays by the bars, squeaking at me.

"It's OK," I say. "Your sister's going to be back soon."

I don't like leaving Venom all lonely, but it's worse not knowing where Vulture is. And even worse than that – what's Brayker gonna do if he finds my rat loose in his flat? I don't really believe that Plum would call pest control. But Brayker would. Straight away.

When I get back downstairs, Ty is waiting outside Brayker's. He's holding a small cage.

"Don't worry," Ty says. "I haven't come to take your friend away. Plum said you might need a little help. This is a bit more secure than a shoe box."

Ty gives Brayker's door a small tap and Plum lets us in. We walk past the kitchen towards the sitting room. Plum opens the door and I see two things at the same time. It's like my eyes don't want to work together.

The first thing I see is Vulture. My rat, who never does anything I say, is standing on two legs, like she's a proper person.

The other thing I see is that this isn't a sitting room. Maybe it was before, but it isn't no more.

It's still got some sitting-room things in it, like a painting on the wall and a fire and some shelves full of books. But right in the middle of it, there's a bed. It's not a normal bed – it's one of them hospital beds with metal sides so the person on it can't fall out.

I think there's an old lady on the bed. I can't see much of her, just tubes and a drip on a pole next to her. Her cover is made from lots of different coloured squares. Some of the squares have got flowers on them, some of them are stripy and there's some gold ones too. A big square in the middle has a star on it. And that's where Vulture is, right in the middle of the star. She looks like she's about to take a bow.

"Here he is," Plum says to the old lady. "My annoying little brother."

The cover moves and I can hear that out-of-breath laughing again.

"Hi, Laurie," Ty says. "How are you doing?"

"Fit as Usain Bolt, Tyrone," the old lady replies. There's more breath and laughing. "Any minute now, I'm going to jump off this bed and race you to Shoreditch Park!"

The laugh sounds like a dog bark. Plum picks up a beaker from the table next to the bed. It's got a lid and a spout, like the ones babies have. I realise that Laurie isn't laughing. She's coughing. Plum helps her take a drink and the way Plum does it, it's like she's done it loads of time before.

"Thank you, Plum," Laurie gasps.

I frown. "Plum?" I say. "You still haven't told me what you're doing here."

"He doesn't know?" Laurie says. Her hand flops onto her chest. "I mustn't laugh. It isn't good for me. But it is funny, Al. All this time and you had no idea that your sister was working here."

Working?

"I do care work," Plum says. "I told you before."

"But not here!" I nearly shout but stop myself. "You didn't tell me you worked here."

"And that's why!" Plum says. "I knew you'd go off on one!"

"Um ..." Ty says. "The clock's ticking, folks!" He scoops Vulture off the bed and into the cage.

"Take your rat back upstairs," Plum says. She puts the beaker back on the table and glares at me. "And don't come back."

Laurie waves her hand and says, "But you haven't introduced me properly yet, Plum. I want to meet the boy who tried to blast me out of my bed with 'Another One Bites The Dust'!"

Plum looks at Laurie, then at me. I feel my cheeks heating up. How was I to know?

Plum sighs. "You heard what Laurie said," she tells me. "Come over here."

I don't want to go closer to the bed. I can see Laurie's hands and they're full of veins. One of the veins has got a needle sticking in it with a tube that goes up to the drip. Her nails have got red polish on them, which looks weird because her fingers are curled up like Vulture's tail.

"Go on," Ty says. "Laurie doesn't bite."

Laurie laughs again. "I haven't got the teeth for that any more."

I take a couple of steps forward. I can see Laurie's chin, then the rest of her face. I blink. Her hair's pink, bright pink. Her face is old and wrinkly, but her hair makes her look like she's shining. Laurie's skin is light brown like Mum's, but Mum's got brown eyes. Laurie's eyes are dark blue.

"What's your friend called?" she asks.

My friend? I wonder.

Ty touches the cage. "This friend."

"This is Vulture," I tell Laurie.

"And very lovely she is too," Laurie says. "Plum tells me that Vulture is not alone. You have two rats?"

"Her sister's called Venom."

"Ahhh," Laurie says. I'm not sure if it's another laugh or a cough. She closes her eyes. Plum's still got her "go away" face on. She waves me towards the door in case I don't understand.

"Sinister Six," Laurie says.

I look at Plum, confused. She shrugs but keeps giving me dagger eyes. I want to go! Venom must be lonely.

"Venom and Vulture are villains," Laurie explains. "Supervillains. In the old *Spiderman* comics. I don't know if anybody reads them any more."

"The girl who had them before me did like *Spiderman* and stuff," I say.

"Well, there you are. Your friends aren't just normal villains, they're supervillains."

That makes me love my rats even more. I want to tell Laurie that Mum named me Al after Dumbledore in Harry Potter. Mum said the first time she held me it was like magic.

"You're welcome to bring Venom and Vulture down any time to see me," Laurie says. "I don't get to make many new friends these days."

Plum's screwed her face into the baddest look I've ever seen from her.

"But my son's going to be home soon," Laurie says. "He's not a great fan of rats, as I believe you know already. So you better be on your way. Check with Plum. She knows the best time to come when Noah's out."

"Your son?" I say.

Laurie's eyes crinkle like she wants to laugh again, but the laugh doesn't come. "Yes, my son."

Brayker has a mum? And she's got pink hair and lives in the sitting room? That's even more weird than Plum opening the door.

And that makes me think. My mum's in prison because Brayker made the guard in the shop stop me, and all this time, Plum's been down here helping Brayker's mum! Plum knew it would upset me if I found out and she still worked here.

Now I know why Plum's staying with me. It's not because she cares about me. It's because it's easier for her to get to work! It's like everyone thinks I'm stupid. They keep secrets and tell me lies and when I find out and get angry, I'm the one who gets told off.

Inside me is hurting and burning and I want to yell. I don't want Laurie to see me shout, because she's not very well. And because Vulture seemed to like her too. I take my deep breaths and hold them in as long as I can. The burning just feels like a bellyache now. I'm still angry, but I can hold it inside.

I take Vulture from Ty and walk out of the room – slap bang into Brayker.

The cage crashes into Brayker's knee. Luckily, I just about manage to keep hold of it. Brayker makes a funny noise. He looks down at Vulture and makes another sound. Brayker's mouth stays open and his eyes are so wide I think they're going to drop out of his head into the cage. He wobbles backwards and his head smacks the hallway wall.

Ty and Plum run out of the sitting room.

"Noah!" Ty shouts. "Are you OK?"

Brayker rubs the back of his head just like the security guard in the shop did, but his eyes don't seem to be looking at any of us.

"Just go, Al!" Plum yells at me. "Now!"

I run upstairs into the flat. I slam the door but don't mean to, because it makes Vulture scared.

She's hunched up in the small cage all trembling. I take her out and hold her in the palm of my hand.

"Sorry," I say to her.

I go into my room and close the door. I put Vulture on my bed. Venom starts chattering in the big cage, pressing her head on the bars.

"OK," I say. "I'll clean it for you."

I take Venom out and she scrabbles up the sides of my duvet onto the bed. She hunches down next to Vulture.

I normally try to clean out a bit of their cage every day, but I forgot for the last two days. I feel bad making my rats live in a smelly home. I'm glad I've got something to do now. I'm not just sitting here waiting for whatever bad thing's gonna happen next.

These are things I've waited for before:

1. I waited for Mum to come out of prison so we could be a real family. She came back and then went again.

2. I waited for Dad to come and take me away from my emergency foster parents. But he said that there wasn't room for me in his third family.

3. I waited with Gran in the prison visiting
    hall, but Mum was too sad to stay with me.

I go and find a bag for my rats' stinky stuff. We
keep Venom and Vulture's straw in the cupboard
under the stairs. There's not much left. Mum told
me to go careful with it until she got her money
and we could buy some more. She made a joke
that the rats were going to be warmer and have
better food than us. I smiled because Mum gave
me one of her real smiles too.

I stop with my hand on the cupboard door. I
can hear sirens. They're getting louder and louder.
Normally, they just pass by, but this time they
don't. They stop.

I creep over to the front door and peek out. An
ambulance has parked up outside the flats. I slam
the door shut again. My heart's beating faster
than Vulture's.

An ambulance. That means someone's been
hurt. Or they're really ill. It could be anyone,
anyone at all. There's loads of people living in this
block and any one of them could be sick.

I stay where I am and listen hard. The door
at the front of the block bangs. The paramedics

must be coming in. It still could be anyone. But ... Laurie's ill. What if she's got worse?

But it's Brayker that I'm really worried about, and the sound his head made when it smacked the wall. What if his skull got cracked? His face went all funny too, like he had a heart attack.

I rub my own heart. Brayker saw Vulture. Then he fell over by himself. No one pushed him. What if that's when his heart stopped working? If Brayker's heart stops, he's dead.

That would mean I killed him.

There's more sirens now, getting louder. The police are coming to arrest me, the same way they arrested Mum in the shop. But this time it's worse. Someone has died.

I go back into my room. I haven't got long. Venom and Vulture have to stay with someone who's going to love them. Ty, of course! He'll make sure they're all right!

"You have to be good for Ty," I say out loud. "He'll be doing us a favour."

Then I realise I can't hear nothing. No chasing, no scuffling, no chattering. Nothing at all.

"Venom? Vulture?" I say.

The police sirens have stopped. My rats haven't moved from the bed. They haven't even moved from the pillow. Venom is snuggled next to Vulture. She turns her head to look at me. Venom's nose twitches, then she rests her head on Vulture's flank.

Vulture doesn't move at all. I swallow hard. I call her name. I take a deep breath and kneel on the floor and stroke her side. I want to feel her breath going in and out. I want to feel her heart.

I can't.

"Vulture," I say. "Stop pretending. I'm not going to hurt you, you know that."

Venom squeaks. She's agreeing with me. Vulture still doesn't move.

"Please, Vulture!"

Maybe if I pick her up and shake her, everything will start working again. But I can't. I don't think Venom will let Vulture go. I lie down on the bed, wrapping my arms around the pillow.

A rat's heart can beat more than four hundred times a minute. If I start counting, maybe Vulture's heart will join in.

"One. Two. Three. Four," I begin.

There's a hard knock on my bedroom door. I try to ignore it.

"Five. Six. Seven."

The door bangs harder. Plum must have brought the police to me. I don't care. I won't stop counting until Vulture's heart starts beating again.

Chapter 11

Vulture

A hand grips my shoulder as I kneel on the floor.

"Al!" It's Plum. "What the hell were you playing at down there? Do you know how much trouble you've caused? It was bad enough that I had to clean that stinky egg off their door last time. Because that was you, wasn't it? Mr Brayker's ..."

I turn and look at her, then back at Vulture. Plum's hand stops gripping so hard but stays on my shoulder.

"Is there something wrong, Al?" she asks.

I open my mouth but can't talk.

"Oh, Al," Plum says. "Is she ...? Oh no! I'm so sorry."

I sniff and look down at Vulture. I want to say that there's nothing to be sorry about. Any moment soon, she's gonna twitch, then jump up and chase Venom under the bed.

But Vulture doesn't. She doesn't move at all. I realise that I've stopped counting. I start again in my head. *One, two, three, four...*

"Are ... are they here?" I say.

"Who?" Plum asks.

Five, six ...

"The police," I say. "To arrest me."

"What police, Al? And why on earth would they arrest you?"

"For what happened to Brayker."

"There's no police, Al." Plum sounds a bit confused. "I know you think Mr Brayker's got it in for you, but he certainly hasn't called the police."

"He's still alive?" I ask.

"When I left him, he was drinking a cup of tea, very much alive."

"I saw an ambulance."

"Yes, that was for him," Plum says. "He had a really bad panic attack and Ty got worried and called the ambulance. He's all right now."

So Brayker's not dead. I should be happy, but I can't stop looking at Vulture. I touch her side. She's not moving at all. I forgot to keep counting again. I can't remember where I got to.

"Fourteen. Fifteen. Sixteen," I say.

"Al? What are you doing?" Plum asks.

"Making Vulture come back! Now I've lost my place again! One! Two! Three!"

Plum's hand leaves my back and she goes away.

Rats' hearts beat much faster, so it might work if I count faster too, but my numbers get all mixed up.

"It hurts, doesn't it?"

It isn't Plum who says this. It's Ty. I didn't even hear him come in. He's kneeling on the floor next to me.

"When my first rat died, it was like I'd lost a member of my family," Ty says. "She was called Flea and I thought she'd live for ever. But most of them don't make three years old. Vulture looks full grown. It was her time. My dad took Flea away without telling me. He said he buried her, but I don't know. I never saw no grave."

"Vulture doesn't need no grave," I tell Ty. "She's coming back."

"I don't want to say this, Al, but Vulture's gone. She isn't coming back. You have to take care of Venom, now. See? Her heart's breaking too."

Venom's face is bent over Vulture. Her whiskers are twitching and she's so close to

Vulture, it looks like Vulture's whiskers are twitching too. Venom's hand is on Vulture's cheek. I pick Venom up and she squeaks at me. I bring her close to my face and bend down so our foreheads rub together. I cradle her close so I can feel her breathe.

"Let's give Vulture a proper send-off," Ty says.

Chapter 12

Brayker

I curl up on my bed with Venom and Vulture.
Venom and I whisper to each other. I tell them how
much I love them and how they make everything
feel all right for me.

I hadn't heard Ty leave, but after a while
there's a gentle knock on my bedroom door and
he's back. Ty's brought my old shoe box, but he's
covered the inside with some red material and put
a cushion in the bottom, made of gold and silver
sparkles. He lifts Vulture up. I want to stop him,
but Venom's squeaking like mad and I have to pick
her up.

Ty nods towards Venom. "She'll want to say
goodbye to her friend too. Bring her along, but
keep her in the small cage."

He puts the box with Vulture down on my bed and lifts the cage towards me. I lower Venom inside. Ty picks up the box, and Venom and me follow him out and down the stairs. Venom isn't saying nothing now. I want to take her out of the cage and cuddle her, but she might jump out of my hands and run away

We go out into the street and cross the road. We pass the shop where Mum was arrested and go into the park.

"What are we going to do?" I say.

"We're going to bury her," Ty replies.

We go past the pond and the playground and walk to the far edge of the park. There's a small path that runs between a group of trees.

Plum is crouching by a tree holding a trowel. Pete is standing behind her. There's a hole dug out between two tree roots.

"Give me Venom," Ty says.

I don't want to. She doesn't really know Ty and she's already upset.

Ty holds out Vulture. "Come on, Al," he says. "You need to do this. It's for Venom's sake."

I give him Venom and take the box containing Vulture. I hug it to me. I realise that Venom has stopped squeaking. My heart jumps and I bend down and peer into the cage. She looks up at me, her whiskers twitching. She's OK.

Plum gives the grave one last pat. "Are you ready, Al?" she asks.

Not really. I don't want to do this, but I have to. Ty brings Venom closer to the hole. I take the lid off the box and look at Vulture.

"She was my best friend," I say.

Ty nods. "I know."

I wrap her in the material that was in the bottom of the box and carefully lift Vulture out. I thought she'd be more floppy, but she's heavy and stiff. I lean over and lay her in the bottom of the hole. Ty brings Venom over so she can see. He picks up a pinch of mud and drops it into the grave.

"You do the same," Ty says to me.

The mud is cold and damp. Maybe that's why no one comes here. It's never in the sunshine. I drop a clump of mud. I don't like the sound it makes when it lands.

Plum starts to scrape the mud back in with the trowel. I watch until I can't see Vulture no more. I take the cushion out of the empty box and hold it close to my face. It still smells of Vulture. Ty lifts Venom's cage towards me so I can hold the cushion close to her. She squeaks and rests her cheek against the bars.

Vulture's grave is nearly filled up. Plum makes sure the top is flat.

"You stay here as long as you like," Plum says to me. "We'll be waiting by the bench over there."

They take Venom with them. It's not far away, but I want Venom with me. She needs me now. I just need to say goodbye. And I do.

"Goodbye, Vulture. Sleep well."

I stand up and that's when I see Brayker. He's walking across the grass towards me. One, two, three steps and he's right by me. We look at each other. Brayker doesn't look like his mum. His eyes are lighter and his face doesn't smile so much.

"I'm sorry, Al," he says.

Brayker's face looks sorry, but I don't believe him. I almost shrug, because I didn't expect him to say that and I don't know what my body should do. Why should he care? He hates rats and he hates me and Mum even more.

"What are you doing here?" I ask.

"Plum told me what happened," Brayker says. "This is a lovely spot for Vulture. No one really comes here."

Inside my head feels like it's full of needles. I
want to cry, but I'm never gonna let Brayker see
me like that.

"You don't care!" I shout. "So don't pretend!"

And suddenly it all explodes out of me.

"How dare you turn up here and pretend to be
my friend!" I shout at Brayker.

And it's not just Brayker! The others must
have told him where we'd be.

I turn to face Ty. "You know it's Brayker's fault
that Mum went back into the shop. If he'd just shut
up, Mum would be here with me now! And I wasn't
even stealing the burgers. I'd really forgotten that
I was holding them."

I spin back towards Brayker. "You've been
trying to make trouble for us from the start. You
complained to the council that Mum's music was
too loud. And now she's back in prison and I can't
be with her. She was so upset she couldn't even
stay with me when I went to see her! And now
Vulture's dead and she was my friend. One of my
only friends."

My mouth stops and I feel all emptied out. I'm
wobbly like it was only crossness that was holding
me together. Then I hear Venom squeaking
like mad. I run over to Ty and grab Venom's

cage. She's running round like she wants to find somewhere to hide. Stupid me! I've just scared her the same way I scared Vulture! I want to take her out and cuddle her, but my fingers don't have the strength to hold her. I put the cage on the ground.

Then I start crying. I don't mean to. I don't want to. But it's like all those angry bubbles that I thought were taking over my brain have burst. And they're full of water. I cry so hard that my throat's hurting. My nose is running too. A hand holds out a tissue. It's Brayker. I ignore it and wipe my face on my sleeve.

"I was in prison too," Brayker says.

I can't help it. I look at him. Brayker's standing as far away as he can, his arm stretched right out to offer me the tissue.

"What?" I say.

It must be another lie, just to get me on his side. Brayker seems to be talking to the bench but loud enough for me to hear.

"It was a long time ago," he says. "It was something stupid that went wrong. So I do understand."

I shake my head. He *must* be lying.

"I was trying to steal some clothes from a shop," Brayker says. "When I was a kid, I lived with

my dad. Mum moved out, but she wasn't far away.
I could choose who I wanted to live with, but … you
know. Boys need their dads and all that."

I don't.

Brayker carries on talking. "Dad worked all
hours to make sure me and my brother were all
right, but it wasn't enough. Not enough for me
anyway. I got fed up of wearing my brother's old
clothes. I wanted new gear, like my mates. So one
day I got the bus into town and went into one of
those big clothes shops on Oxford Street. I grabbed
a load of shirts that were closest to the shop door
and ran."

I wait for Brayker to keep going. Even Venom
is looking out at him.

"I ran straight into the road and in front of a
car."

I realise my hand is clapped to my mouth, even
when I can see that Brayker didn't die. And he
doesn't walk like he got injured.

"The car swerved to miss me," Brayker says
in a low voice. "But it hit a woman cycling past
instead. She was from round here. She'd been in
my brother's year at school."

Ty touches Brayker's shoulder. "But they told
you she made a good recovery, didn't they, Noah?"

"Yes." Brayker's voice is so quiet I have to lean forward to hear him. "But … just seeing her lying on the ground, not moving …" He shakes his head. "It was all my fault."

I say, "Did you go to prison for hurting her?"

He shakes his head. "No, because that was an accident. I was in prison for stealing the clothes." He gives a weird laugh. It's the laugh people make when something isn't funny. "The thing is, I wouldn't even have worn those kind of shirts. They were the ones you wear if you work in an office and I definitely wasn't working in an office.

"I was too young for proper prison. I was sent to what they called 'borstal' back then. It was only for a few weeks, but some of the boys there were terrors – it was like a training school for bullies. No one came to visit me and when I came home … my dad and brother didn't want anything to do with me. They were ashamed. We got our windows broken a couple of times and eggs chucked at our door."

I take a big gulp of air.

"You were only sixteen," Ty says. "A lad."

"Yes," Brayker says. "I was, but Dad still threw me out."

"Did you go to your mum?" I ask.

"Yes, but it didn't work. It was like I wanted to take out all my anger on her. Once, Mum said I couldn't go out, and I went into the kitchen and smashed anything I knew would break. After that, I ended up in a children's home. I was so angry ..."

I rub my face. I think about the times I feel like I've got angry bubbles pushing each other around inside my head.

"Most of the children in there were angry too," Brayker says. "We'd go out on stealing trips. We'd steal sweets, clothes, records, anything. We didn't even need the stuff. We were our own little gang. And most of us ended up in and out of borstal for the next few years. I moved around a lot, but it was hard to settle anywhere. As soon as I said I'd been in prison, folks didn't want to know me."

"If you've been in prison," I say, "you shouldn't have been so nasty to Mum."

"I try to keep myself to myself," Brayker says, "but I grew up round here. Some of the folks who've been here a long time don't forget. And they don't forgive. You know the small supermarket?"

I nod. "The one with the man outside who looks at everyone?"

"They won't serve me in there because the girl who got hit by the car – her son owns it now. He told me I'm not welcome. And he tells anyone else who's willing to listen what I did to his mum. I thought maybe your mum knew and that's why she was playing her music so loud. It wouldn't be the first time that a stranger's made me suffer." Brayker looks at me. "I just wanted to start again."

"So why didn't you go somewhere else?" I say. Brayker's grown up. He doesn't have to do what he's told if he doesn't like it. He can go wherever he wants.

"Because of Mum," he says.

Laurie, the old woman with the bright pink hair. I still can't believe that she's Brayker's mum.

"She's got bad lungs," Brayker says. "I did move away for a long time but came back when Mum knew she wasn't going to get better. My dad passed away ten years ago and my brother lives in Germany. I knew that it was my turn to do my best for Mum. But it's been hard. When I came back, I didn't dare go out much. If it wasn't for Pete and Ty bringing us food, I don't know what I'd have done. It makes a difference when someone cares about you."

Brayker's holding a plastic bag. He reaches inside it and brings out some flowers, three small red ones. Brayker goes over to Vulture's grave and lays the flowers on top. Then he straightens up and rubs his back.

"Ready to go?" Ty asks me.

No, I don't think I ever will be, but I reach out, touch the pile of earth and whisper, "Vulture."

Then I turn to Brayker. "Vulture cared about me," I say.

"I know," he says.

Chapter 13

Venom and Vulture and Mum and Me and Laurie and Plum and ... Everyone

Mum has to stay in prison for another few weeks, but I'm allowed to stay at home with Plum. She can't be with me all the time as she has to go to college and do her care work, so sometimes Gran comes round to check up on me. I know that I don't always behave the way that people want me to, but I'm trying really hard to not be angry all the time. I think it's working, mostly. Sometimes it's hard because Gran can be very annoying. Especially when she tells me off about my manners or the state of my bedroom.

When I'm feeling stressed, I go down and see Laurie. If Brayker's not there, I bring Venom with me. It feels good to have another friend, even if it's a strange old lady with bright pink hair. When Brayker's at home, he makes us all tea. We still don't have much to say to each other, but sitting in silence doesn't feel bad.

I write Mum a letter, telling her that I've made friends. I want her to know that when she comes out of prison we'll be OK. We can be sad and happy and scared together. Gran wants to take some photos to send to Mum, but it doesn't feel right if Vulture isn't in them. So I draw a picture for her. In it, Mum's hugging me and smiling. Vulture's looking down from Heaven and Venom's on my shoulder looking up. Plum is there – and Ty and Pete and Laurie. Then I feel bad and draw in a tiny Brayker. I make my arms really long so I can reach around all of them.

Author spotlight

Patrice Lawrence is an award-winning writer of stories for children and young people. Her books for young adults include *Orangeboy*, shortlisted for the Costa Children's Book Award, and winner of the Bookseller YA Prize and Waterstones Prize for Older Children's Fiction; *Indigo Donut*; *Rose, Interrupted* and *Eight Pieces of Silva*. She has also written for younger readers – *Diver's Daughter* is inspired by British Black history. *Toad Attack* is inspired by – um – flying frogs. Prior to becoming a full-time writer, Patrice worked for the voluntary sector promoting social justice, equality and inclusion.

Background to the novel

Prison

Prisons feature in the novel because Al's mum has previously spent time in prison and is sent back to prison when an attempt at shoplifting leads to a scuffle with a security guard.

There are around 90,000 people in prison in the UK. Of these, only around 4,000 are women. It has been estimated that more than 300,000 children in the UK have a parent in prison, and every week 10,000 children visit a parent in prison.

Although prisoners are allowed visits from friends and family, there are strict rules that they must follow; for example, all visitors must be searched before they enter the prison. Usually, prisoners must sit down throughout the visit; they are not allowed to stand up or move around while their visitors are with them. Visitors may briefly hug or kiss the prisoner only at the very start or the very end of the visit.

People face lots of problems when they are released from prison; for example, finding somewhere to live can be very difficult. Some become homeless because they cannot find a place to live. Many ex-prisoners find it very difficult to get a job. These problems can lead to people committing another crime; almost half of prisoners released from prison commit another crime within a year.

Borstals

Towards the end of the novel, it is revealed that Brayker was arrested for shoplifting and sent to a borstal in his teenage years. Until 1982, all prisoners below the age of 21 were sent to special prisons known as borstals. Borstals had strict discipline and a strict routine of physical exercise, school lessons and training to help the prisoners get a job when they were released. This routine filled eight hours every day. Bullying and violence often occurred. Since 1982, young offenders have been placed in young offender institutions, secure training centres or children's homes, instead of borstals.

Rats

Al's closest and only friends in the novel are his two pet rats, Venom and Vulture, but rats have a poor reputation. They can often be seen scavenging in food waste and are thought to carry and spread disease. They have long been blamed for causing the Bubonic plague, the worst outbreak of which occurred in the fourteenth century and was known as the Black Death, as they carry fleas which bite and infect humans. In fact, rats are very clean animals and are less likely to carry diseases than cats.

Rats can grow as long as 45cm from the tip of their nose to the end of their tail but can squeeze through a hole that is just 2cm wide. They have extremely sharp teeth that can bite through plastic, glass and even some metals. However, as with most animals, they only bite a human when they are frightened or feel threatened. When bought from good pet shops, rats can make excellent pets because they are friendly, highly intelligent and easy to train.

Who's who in this novel?

Al lives with his mum in a flat on a tower block estate in London. They have moved home a lot of times, so Al has no friends and finds school difficult. He takes comfort in his pet rats, named Venom and Vulture.

Ramona is Al's mum. She has been recently released from prison, has no job and little money. This makes it very difficult for her to provide food for her son and so she is driven to shoplifting.

Gran is Al's grandmother and Ramona's mother. She often steps in to help Ramona and Al but is quite strict and always ready to give her opinion on her grandson's poor behaviour.

Plum is Al's half sister as they have the same father but different mothers. She studies at college and has a job as a carer. When Ramona is sent back to prison, Plum comes to look after Al.

Al's dad has three families. The first was with Plum's mother and the second with Al's mum. Al has not seen his dad for three years. Although he was sent to stay with his dad when he was younger, his dad now has a new family and says his new partner is too busy with their twins to look after Al.

Noah Brayker and his mother, Laurie, live in the flat below Al and Ramona's flat. Al hates Mr Brayker because he complained about Ramona's loud music, and Al thinks he is to blame for her being sent back to prison.

Ty and Pete live in a flat on the same estate as Al, Ramona and Mr Brayker. They do lots of things to help the people on the estate, including cooking food for them and even delivering it to their doors.

What to read next

High Rise Mystery by Sharna Jackson

When their art teacher is murdered on their tower-block estate, sisters Nik and Norva turn into detectives to solve the crime. As they collect clues and examine methods and motives, their investigation takes a worrying turn. A fast, funny and gripping story.

Cowgirl by G. R. Gemin

Growing up on the Bryn Mawr Estate in South Wales, all Gemma sees are burglaries and boredom. But when the legendary Cowgirl arrives abruptly in Gemma's life, it turns out they both have a mission on their hands. It's been a long time since anyone on the Bryn Mawr Estate ever saw a cow. But they're about to get a lot closer to home.

What do you think?

1. Al loves his pet rats, Venom and Vulture.
    Why do you think Al feels so close to them?
    What are some of the reasons you would
    have a pet rat?

2. In the novel, Al decides to take revenge on
    his neighbour, Mr Brayker. Do you think Mr
    Brayker deserves to be so hated by Al? Give
    three reasons to explain why or why not.

3. If you were Al, who would you choose to live
    with: Mum, Dad, Gran, or Plum? Why?

4. Think about all of the different adults you meet
    in the novel. Do you admire or respect any
    of them? What advice would you give each of
    them?

5. What do you think Al has learned about life by
    the end of the novel?

Quick quiz

When you have finished reading *Rat*, answer these questions to see how much you can remember about the novel. The answers are on page 147.

1. What food is Al dreaming of eating at the very beginning of the novel?

2. How many different families does Al's dad have?

3. When Al and his mum moved to the estate, Mr Brayker phoned the council to complain. What was he complaining about?

4. What does Al's mum try to shoplift from their local shop?

5. After playing his music really loudly, what is Al's next act of revenge against his neighbour, Mr Brayker?

6. What is the best food to tempt a rat out from under your fridge?

7. What television programme are Ty and Pete watching when Al first visits their flat?

8. What is the name of Mr Brayker's mother?

9. Where do Al, Plum and Ty bury Vulture?

10. What is unusual about the way that Al draws himself at the very end of the novel?

Word list

back bend: *(slang)* effort, hard work

borstal: a prison for young people

drip: a piece of medical equipment that is used to put liquid into a person's veins

hooked: to catch with a hook; can also mean addicted

mussed up: *(informal)* untidy or messy

rat: a rodent, similar to a large mouse; also an insult, e.g. *You little rat!*; also to reveal incriminating information, e.g. *He refused to rat on his friends.*

reception: a building or desk where visitors to a hotel, office or prison are greeted

screwface: *(slang)* a screwed-up face expressing anger

venom: a poisonous liquid produced by some snakes, scorpions, etc; also the name of one of Al's pet rats

vulture: a bird of prey that feeds on dead animals; also the name of one of Al's pet rats

wasteman: *(slang)* a person who wastes their life

Quick quiz answers

1. Cornflakes, milk and sugar

2. Three

3. The loud music that Al's mum was playing

4. Cheese

5. He breaks an egg on Mr Brayker's front door

6. Sweetcorn, Coco Pops or chocolate (although chocolate is not good for rats)

7. *Countdown*

8. Laurie

9. In the local park

10. He draws himself with really long arms

Super-Readable
ROLLERCOASTERS

Super-Readable Rollercoasters are an exciting new collection brought to you through a collaboration between Oxford University Press and specialist publisher Barrington Stoke. Written by bestselling and award-winning authors, these titles are intended to engage and enthuse, with themes and issues matched to the readers' age.

The books have been expertly edited to remove any barriers to comprehension and then carefully laid out in Barrington Stoke's dyslexia-friendly font to make them as accessible as possible. Their shorter length allows readers to build confidence and reading stamina while engaging in a gripping, well-told story that will ensure an enjoyable reading experience.

**Other titles available in the
Super-Readable Rollercoasters series:**

Edgar & Adolf by Phil Earle and Michael Wagg
Lightning Strike by Tanya Landman
I Am The Minotaur by Anthony McGowan
Dark Peak by Marcus Sedgwick

Free online teaching resources accompany all the titles in the Super-Readable Rollercoasters series and are available from:

http://www.oxfordsecondary.com/superreadable